ANIMAL

STORIES

For Ted, who helped us make this book
Andrew & Michael

KINGFISHER
An imprint of Kingfisher Publications Plc
New Penderel House, 283-288 High Holborn
London WC1V 7HZ
www.kingfisherpub.com

First published by Kingfisher 1999
2 4 6 8 10 9 7 5 3 1

A CIP catalogue record for this book is available from the British Library.

ISBN 0 7534 1010 9

Printed in India

2TR/0804/THOM/MA/80HIB/F

1TS/0904/THOM/MA/80HIB/F

ANIMAL STORIES

CHOSEN BY

MICHAEL MORPURGO

ILLUSTRATED BY

ANDREW DAVIDSON

CONTENTS

INTRODUCTION

IT IS A STRANGE PHENOMENON, but the more urban our lives become the more we seem to be fascinated by the wildlife that surrounds us. For most of us now, the world of nature, of animals, of the outdoors is brought to us by television. The lives of otters, of elephants, of pelicans, of the badger and the rat are brought right into our sitting rooms. They come to us. We see them second-hand, through a glass, distantly. In all the history of mankind we have never been so isolated from the natural world around us, yet at the same time we are still entranced by it. I think I know why.

I think we yearn to feel close to our fellow creatures. We long to feel we are part of their world, not mere observers. Certainly that is true for me. I am lucky enough to live and work in the heart of the countryside. As I write this, sheep are shifting in the field beyond my window, policed by foraging crows, a blue tit clings upside down in the thatch searching for insects in the straw, a whirl of starlings unfolds in the wind and is buffeted away over Innocents' Copse. I have only to put on my boots and walk down the high-hedged lane towards the Torridge river to see where the badger has passed on his way last night up his alleyway through the field hedge. My nose tells me a fox has been by even more recently. Down by the river I might see a heron lifting off and lumbering skywards, and I might hear the slap of a leaping salmon and the plop of a water rat. If I'm lucky, I'll spot a kingfisher flashing by, straight as a jewelled arrow – gone before I saw it. And if I'm very silent, still and patient, I might know that moment again when an otter came up out of the river and saw me sitting there. He did not run away. We just met. And when tonight I go milking under a star-filled heaven, the vixen will cry at me and the tawny owl will let me know he's there and watching, and I'll feel part of it all, just one of them.

It has been such a joy to gather this selection of stories together, to discover new voices and to hear once again voices I had almost forgotten – to me a story on the page is a told thing, a sounding thing. I have just chosen what I love, that's all there is to it. Certainly there is a unifying theme in the collection – the animal world we live in and are part of. But the writers relate to this world in a multiplicity of ways, seeking always to understand it better, to discover or explain the elemental connections between man and beast and planet. There are of course naturalistic stories of animal life, but there are anthropomorphic folk tales, too, scientific recording, stories that concern the emotional ties we have with nature and animals, our interreliance, our shared existence. So look for no coherent pattern, look just for wonderful storytelling and fine writing, inspired in each case by the writer's intense closeness to his subject, by his intense knowledge and love of it. It is that that draws us in, brings us close again to our fellowship with the world around us and the creatures that inhabit it.

Michael Morpurgo
Devon, June 1999

THE BIRDS BEGAN TO SING

JANET FRAME

To begin: an exquisite prose poem about seeing, about listening, about being, by a wonderful writer best known for her autobiography, An Angel at My Table. *She felt life keenly, and spent many long years searching for "the name of the song".*

THE BIRDS BEGAN TO SING. There were four and twenty of them singing, and they were blackbirds.

And I said, what are you singing all day and night, in the sun and the dark and the rain, and in the wind that turns the tops of the trees silver?

We are singing, they said. We are singing and we have just begun, and we've a long way to sing, and we can't stop, we've got to go on and on. Singing.

The birds began to sing.

I put on my coat and I walked in the rain over the hills. I walked through swamps full of red water, and down gullies covered in snowberries, and then up gullies again, with snow grass growing there, and speargrass, and over creeks near flax and tussock and manuka.

I saw a pine tree on top of a hill.

I saw a skylark dipping and rising.

I saw it was snowing somewhere over the hills, but not where I was.

I stood on a hill and looked and looked.

I wasn't singing. I tried to sing but I couldn't think of the song.

So I went back home to the boarding house where I live, and I sat on the stairs in the front and I listened. I listened with my head and my eyes and my brain and my hands. With my body.

The birds began to sing.

They were blackbirds sitting on the telegraph wires and hopping on the apple trees. There were four and twenty of them singing.

What is the song? I said. Tell me the name of the song.

I am a human being and I read books and I hear music and I like to see things in print. I like to see *vivace andante* words by music by performed by written for. So I said what is the name of the song, tell me and I will write it and you can listen at my window when I get the finest musicians in the country to play it, and you will feel so nice to hear your song so tell me the name.

They stopped singing. It was dark outside although the sun was shining. It was dark and there was no more singing.

THE SNOW GOOSE

PAUL GALLICO

I have always loved this story. Rhayader is a recluse, seen and feared as an ogre by local children, until one of them, Frith, dares to bring a wounded snow goose to the lighthouse where he lives – for he is known to care for all wild things.

ONE NOVEMBER AFTERNOON, three years after Rhayader had come to the Great Marsh, a child approached the lighthouse studio by means of the sea wall. In her arms she carried a burden.

She was no more than twelve, slender, dirty, nervous and timid as a bird, but beneath the grime as eerily beautiful as a marsh faery. She was pure Saxon, large-boned, fair, with a head to which her body was yet to grow, and deep-set, violet-coloured eyes.

She was desperately frightened of the ugly man she had come to see, for legend had already begun to gather about Rhayader, and the native wild-fowlers hated him for interfering with their sport.

But greater than her fear was the need of that which she bore. For locked in her child's heart was the knowledge, picked up somewhere in the swampland, that this ogre who lived in the lighthouse had magic that could heal injured things.

She had never seen Rhayader before and was close to fleeing in panic at the dark apparition that appeared at the studio door, drawn by her footsteps – the black head and beard, the sinister hump and the crooked claw.

She stood there staring, poised like a disturbed marsh bird for instant flight.

But his voice was deep and kind when he spoke to her.

"What is it, child?"

She stood her ground, and then edged timidly forward. The thing she carried in her arms was a large white bird, and it was quite still. There were stains of blood on its whiteness and on her kirtle where she had held it to her.

The girl placed it in his arms. "I found it, sir. It's hurted. Is it still alive?"

"Yes. Yes, I think so. Come in, child, come in."

Rhayader went inside, bearing the bird, which he placed upon a table, where it moved feebly. Curiosity overcame fear. The girl followed and found herself in a room warmed by a coal fire, shining with many coloured pictures that covered the walls, and full of a strange but pleasant smell.

The bird fluttered. With his good hand Rhayader spread one of its immense white pinions. The end was beautifully tipped with black.

Rhayader looked and marvelled, and said: "Child! where did you find it?"

"In t' marsh, sir, where fowlers had been. What – what is it, sir?"

"It's a snow goose from Canada. But how in all heaven came it here?"

The name seemed to mean nothing to the little girl. Her deep violet eyes, shining out of the dirt on her thin face, were fixed with concern on the injured bird.

She said: "Can 'ee heal it, sir?"

"Yes, yes," said Rhayader. "We will try. Come, you shall help me."

There were scissors and bandages and splints on a shelf, and he was marvellously deft, even with the crooked claw that managed to hold things.

He said: "Ah, she has been shot, poor thing. Her leg is broken, and the wing tip! but not badly. See, we will clip her primaries, so that we can bandage it, but in the spring the feathers will grow and she will be able to fly again. We'll bandage it close to her body, so that she cannot move it until it has set, and then make a splint for the poor leg."

Her fears forgotten, the child watched, fascinated, as he worked, and all the more so because while he fixed a fine splint to the shattered leg he told her the most wonderful story.

The bird was a young one, no more than a year old. She was born in a northern land far, far across the seas, a land belonging to England. Flying to the south to escape the snow and ice and bitter cold, a great storm had seized her and whirled and buffeted her about. It was a truly terrible storm, stronger than her great wings, stronger than anything. For days and nights it held her in its grip and there was nothing she could do but fly before it. When finally it had blown itself out and her sure instincts took her south again, she was over different land and surrounded by strange birds that she had never seen before. At last, exhausted by her ordeal, she had sunk to rest in a friendly green marsh, only to be met by the blast from the hunter's gun.

"A bitter reception for a visiting princess," concluded Rhayader. "We will call her *'La Princesse Perdue'*, the Lost Princess. And in a few days she will be feeling much better.

See!" He reached into his pocket and produced a handful of grain. The snow goose opened its round yellow eyes and nibbled at it.

The child laughed with delight, and then suddenly caught her breath with alarm as the full import of where she was pressed in upon her, and without a word she turned and fled out of the door.

"Wait, wait!" cried Rhayader, and went to the entrance, where he stopped so that it framed his dark bulk. The girl was already fleeing down the sea wall, but she paused at his voice and looked back.

"What is your name, child?"

"Frith."

"Eh?" said Rhayader. "Fritha, I suppose. Where do you live?"

"Wi' t' fisherfolk at Wickaeldroth." She gave the name the old Saxon pronunciation.

"Will you come back tomorrow, or the next day, to see how the Princess is getting along?"

She paused, and again Rhayader must have thought of the wild water birds caught motionless in that split second of alarm before they took to flight.

But her thin voice came back to him: "Ay!"

And then she was gone, with her fair hair streaming out behind her.

The snow goose mended rapidly and by mid-winter was already limping about the enclosure with the wild pink-footed geese with which it associated, rather than the barnacles, and had learned to come to be fed at Rhayader's call. And the child, Fritha, or Frith, was a frequent visitor. She had overcome her fear of Rhayader. Her imagination was captured by the presence of this strange white princess from a land far over the sea, a land that was all pink, as she knew from the map that Rhayader showed her, and on which they traced the stormy path of the lost bird from its home in Canada to the Great Marsh of Essex.

Then one June morning a group of late pink-feet, fat and well fed from the winter at the lighthouse, answered the stronger call of the breeding-grounds and rose lazily, climbing into the sky in ever-widening circles. With them, her white body and black-tipped pinions shining in the spring sun, was the snow goose. It so happened that Frith was at the lighthouse. Her cry brought Rhayader running from the studio.

"Look! Look! The Princess! Be she going away?"

Rhayader stared into the sky at the climbing specks. "Ay," he said, unconsciously dropping into her manner of speech. "The Princess is going home. Listen! she is bidding us farewell."

Out of the clear sky came the mournful barking of the pink-feet, and above it the higher, clearer note of the snow goose. The specks drifted northward, formed into a tiny v, diminished, and vanished.

With the departure of the snow goose ended the visits of Frith to the lighthouse. Rhayader learned all over again the meaning of the word "loneliness".

That summer, out of his memory, he painted a picture of a slender, grime-covered child, her fair hair blown by a November storm, who bore in her arms a wounded white bird.

In mid-October the miracle occurred. Rhayader was in his enclosure, feeding his birds. A grey north-east wind was blowing and the land was sighing beneath the incoming tide. Above the sea and the wind noises he heard a clear, high note. He turned his eyes upward to the evening sky in time to see first an infinite speck, then a black-and-white pinioned dream that circled the lighthouse once, and

N
S
W

finally a reality that dropped to earth in the pen and came waddling forward importantly to be fed, as though she had never been away. It was the snow goose. There was no mistaking her. Tears of joy came to Rhayader's eyes. Where had she been? Surely not home to Canada. No, she must have summered in Greenland or Spitzbergen with the pink-feet. She had remembered and had returned.

When next Rhayader went into Chelmbury for supplies, he left a message with the postmistress – one that must have caused her much bewilderment. He said: "Tell Frith, who lives with the fisherfolk at Wickaeldroth, that the Lost Princess has returned."

Three days later, Frith, taller, still tousled and unkempt, came shyly to the lighthouse to visit *La Princesse Perdue*.

Time passed. On the Great Marsh it was marked by the height of the tides, the slow march of the season, the passage of the birds, and, for Rhayader, by the arrival and departure of the snow goose.

The world outside boiled and seethed and rumbled with the eruption that was soon to break forth and come close to marking its destruction. But not yet did it touch upon Rhayader, or, for that matter, Frith. They had fallen into a curious natural rhythm, even as the child grew older. When the snow goose was at the lighthouse, then she came, too, to visit and learn many things from Rhayader. They sailed together in his speedy boat, that he handled so skilfully. They caught wildfowl for the ever-increasing colony, and built new pens and enclosures for them. From him she learned the lore of every wild bird, from gull to gyrfalcon, that flew the marshes. She cooked for him sometimes, and even learned to mix his paints.

But when the snow goose returned to its summer home it was as though some kind of bar was up between them, and she did not come to the lighthouse. One year the bird did not return, and Rhayader was heartbroken. All things seemed to have ended for him. He painted furiously through the winter and the next summer, and never once saw the child. But in the fall the familiar cry once more rang from the sky, and the huge white bird, now at its full growth, dropped from the skies as mysteriously as it had departed. Joyously, Rhayader sailed his boat into Chelmbury and left his message with the postmistress.

Curiously, it was more than a month after he had left the message before Frith reappeared at the lighthouse, and Rhayader, with a shock, realized that she was a child no longer.

After the year in which the bird had remained away, its periods of absence grew shorter and shorter. It had grown so tame that it followed Rhayader about and even came into the studio while he was working.

In the spring of 1940 the birds migrated early from the Great Marsh. The world was on fire. The whine and roar of the bombers and the thudding explosions frightened them. The first day of May, Frith and Rhayader stood shoulder to shoulder on the sea wall and watched the last of the unpinioned pink-feet and barnacle geese rise from their sanctuary; she, tall, slender, free as air and hauntingly beautiful; he, dark, grotesque, his massive bearded head raised to the sky, his glowing eyes watching the geese form their flight tracery.

"Look, Philip," Frith said.

Rhayader followed her eyes. The snow goose had taken flight, her giant wings spread, but she was flying low, and once came quite close to them, so that for a moment the spreading black-tipped, white pinions seemed to caress them and they felt the rush of the bird's swift passage. Once, twice, she circled the lighthouse, then dropped to earth again in the enclosure with the pinioned geese and commenced to feed.

"She be'ent going," said Frith, with marvel in her voice. The bird in its close passage seemed to have woven a kind of magic about her. "The Princess be goin' t' stay."

"Ay," said Rhayader, and his voice was shaken too. "She'll stay. She will never go away again. The Lost Princess is lost no more. This is her home now – of her own free will."

The spell the bird had girt about her was broken, and Frith was suddenly conscious of the fact that she was frightened, and the things that frightened her were in Rhayader's eyes – the longing and the loneliness and the deep, welling, unspoken things that lay in and behind them as he turned them upon her.

His last words were repeating themselves in her head as though he had said them again: "This is her home now – of her own free will." The delicate tendrils of her instincts reached to him and carried to her the message of the things he could not speak because of what he felt himself to be, mis-shapen and grotesque. And where his voice might have soothed her, her fright grew greater at his silence and the power of the unspoken things between them. The woman in her bade her take flight from something that she was not yet capable of understanding.

Frith said: "I – I must go. Goodbye. I be glad the – the Princess will stay. You'll not be so alone now."

She turned and walked swiftly away, and his sadly spoken "Goodbye, Frith," was only a half-heard ghost of a sound borne to her ears above the rustling of the marsh grass. She was far away before she dared turn for a backward glance. He was still standing on the sea wall, a dark speck against the sky.

Her fear had stilled now. It had been replaced by

something else, a queer sense of loss that made her stand quite still for a moment, so sharp was it. Then, more slowly, she continued on, away from the skyward-pointing finger of the lighthouse and the man beneath it.

THE HAPPY PRINCE

OSCAR WILDE

Here, in one of my favourite stories, everyone speaks: the townspeople, the statue of the Happy Prince – even the Swallow. Wilde thereby weaves the most tragic and touching of fairy tales, which uses an animal to tell us so much about ourselves.

HIGH ABOVE THE CITY, on a tall column, stood the statue of the Happy Prince. He was gilded all over with thin leaves of fine gold, for eyes he had two bright sapphires, and a large red ruby glowed on his sword-hilt.

He was very much admired indeed. "He is as beautiful as a weathercock," remarked one of the Town Councillors who wished to gain a reputation for having artistic tastes; "only not quite so useful," he added, fearing lest people should think him unpractical, which he really was not.

"Why can't you be like the Happy Prince?" asked a sensible mother of her little boy who was crying for the moon. "The Happy Prince never dreams of crying for anything."

"I am glad there is someone in the world who is quite

happy," muttered a disappointed man as he gazed at the wonderful statue.

"He looks just like an angel," said the Charity Children as they came out of the cathedral in their bright scarlet cloaks and their clean white pinafores.

"How do you know?" said the Mathematical Master, "you have never seen one."

"Ah! but we have, in our dreams," answered the children; and the Mathematical Master frowned and looked very severe, for he did not approve of children dreaming.

One night there flew over the city a little Swallow. His friends had gone away to Egypt six weeks before, but he had stayed behind, for he was in love with the most beautiful Reed. He had met her early in the spring as he was flying down the river after a big yellow moth, and had been so attracted by her slender waist that he had stopped to talk to her.

"Shall I love you?" said the Swallow, who liked to come to the point at once, and the Reed made him a low bow. So he flew round and round her, touching the water with his wings, and making silver ripples. This was his courtship, and it lasted all through the summer.

"It is a ridiculous attachment," twittered the other Swallows; "she has no money, and far too many relations"; and indeed the river was quite full of Reeds. Then, when the autumn came they all flew away.

After they had gone he felt lonely, and began to tire of his lady-love. "She has no conversation," he said, "and I am afraid that she is a coquette, for she is always flirting with the wind." And certainly, whenever the wind blew, the Reed made the most graceful curtseys. "I admit that she is domestic," he continued, "but I love travelling, and my wife, consequently, should love travelling also."

"Will you come away with me?" he said finally to her; but the Reed shook her head, she was so attached to her home.

"You have been trifling with me," he cried. "I am off to the Pyramids. Goodbye!" and he flew away.

All day long he flew, and at night-time he arrived at the city. "Where shall I put up?" he said; "I hope the town has made preparations."

Then he saw the statue on the tall column.

"I will put up there," he cried; "it is a fine position, with plenty of fresh air." So he alighted just between the feet of the Happy Prince.

"I have a golden bedroom," he said softly to himself as he looked round, and he prepared to go to sleep; but just as he was putting his head under his wing a large drop of water fell on him. "What a curious thing!" he cried; "there is not a single cloud in the sky, the stars are quite clear and bright, and yet it is raining. The climate in the north of Europe is really dreadful. The Reed used to like the rain, but that was merely her selfishness."

Then another drop fell.

"What is the use of a statue if it cannot keep the rain off?" he said; "I must look for a good chimney-pot," and he determined to fly away.

But before he had opened his wings, a third drop fell, and he looked up, and saw – Ah! what did he see?

The eyes of the Happy Prince were filled with tears, and tears were running down his golden cheeks. His face was so beautiful in the moonlight that the little Swallow was filled with pity.

"Who are you?" he said.

"I am the Happy Prince."

"Why are you weeping then?" asked the Swallow; "you have quite drenched me."

"When I was alive and had a human heart," answered the statue, "I did not know what tears were, for I lived in the Palace of Sans-Souci, where sorrow is not allowed to enter. In the daytime I played with my companions in the garden, and in the evening I led the dance in the Great Hall. Round the garden ran a very lofty wall, but I never cared to ask what lay beyond it, everything about me was so beautiful. My courtiers called me the Happy Prince, and happy indeed I was, if pleasure be happiness. So I lived, and so I died. And now that I am dead they have set me up here so high that I can see all the ugliness and all the misery of my city, and though my heart is made of lead yet I cannot choose but weep."

"What! is he not solid gold?" said the Swallow to himself. He was too polite to make any personal remarks out loud.

"Far away," continued the statue in a low musical voice, "far away in a little street there is a poor house. One of the windows is open, and through it I can see a woman seated at a table. Her face is thin and worn, and she has coarse, red hands, all pricked by the needle, for she is a seamstress. She is embroidering passion-flowers on a satin gown for the loveliest of the Queen's maids-of-honour to wear at the next Court-ball. In a bed in the corner of the room her little boy is lying ill. He has a fever, and is asking for oranges. His mother has nothing to give him but river water, so he is crying. Swallow, Swallow, little Swallow, will you not bring her the ruby out of my sword-hilt? My feet are fastened to this pedestal and I cannot move."

"I am waited for in Egypt," said the Swallow. "My friends are flying up and down the Nile, and talking to the large lotus-flowers. Soon they will go to sleep in the tomb of the great King. The King is there himself in his painted coffin. He is wrapped in yellow linen, and embalmed with spices. Round his neck is a chain of pale green jade, and his hands are like withered leaves."

"Swallow, Swallow, little Swallow," said the Prince, "will you not stay with me for one night, and be my messenger? The boy is so thirsty, and the mother so sad."

"I don't think I like boys," answered the Swallow. "Last summer, when I was staying on the river, there were two rude boys, the miller's sons, who were always throwing stones at me. They never hit me, of course; we swallows fly far too well for that, and besides, I come of a family famous for its agility; but still, it was a mark of disrespect."

But the Happy Prince looked so sad that the little Swallow was sorry. "It is very cold here," he said; "but I will stay with you for one night, and be your messenger."

"Thank you, little Swallow," said the Prince.

So the Swallow picked out the great ruby from the Prince's sword, and flew away with it in his beak over the roofs of the town.

He passed by the cathedral tower, where the white marble angels were sculptured. He passed by the palace and heard the sound of dancing. A beautiful girl came out on the balcony with her lover. "How wonderful the stars are," he said to her, "and how wonderful is the power of love!"

"I hope my dress will be ready in time for the State-ball," she answered; "I have ordered passion-flowers to be embroidered on it; but the seamstresses are so lazy."

He passed over the river, and saw the lanterns hanging to the masts of the ships. He passed over the Ghetto, and saw the old Jews bargaining with each other, and weighing out money in copper scales. At last he came to the poor house and looked in. The boy was tossing feverishly on his bed, and the mother had fallen asleep, she was so tired. In he hopped, and laid the great ruby on the table beside the woman's thimble. Then he flew gently round the bed, fanning the boy's forehead with his wings. "How cool I feel," said the boy, "I must be getting better"; and he sank into a delicious slumber.

Then the Swallow flew back to the Happy Prince, and told him what he had done. "It is curious," he remarked, "but I feel quite warm now, although it is so cold."

"That is because you have done a good action," said the Prince. And the little swallow began to think, and then he fell asleep. Thinking always made him sleepy.

When day broke he flew down to the river and had a bath. "What a remarkable phenomenon," said the Professor of Ornithology as he was passing over the bridge. "A swallow in winter!" And he wrote a long letter about it to the local newspaper. Everyone quoted it, it was full of so many words that they could not understand.

"Tonight I go to Egypt," said the Swallow, and he was in high spirits at the prospect. He visited all the public monuments, and sat a long time on top of the church steeple. Wherever he went the Sparrows chirruped, and said to each other, "What a distinguished stranger!" so he enjoyed himself very much.

When the moon rose he flew back to the Happy Prince. "Have you any commissions for Egypt?" he cried; "I am just starting."

"Swallow, Swallow, little Swallow," said the Prince, "will you not stay with me one night longer?"

"I am waited for in Egypt," answered the Swallow." Tomorrow my friends will fly up to the Second Cataract. The river-horse couches there among the bulrushes, and on a great granite throne sits the God Memnon. All night long he watches the stars, and when the morning star shines he utters one cry of joy, and then he is silent. At noon the yellow lions come down to the water's edge to drink. They have eyes like green beryls, and their roar is louder than the roar of the cataract."

"Swallow, Swallow, little Swallow," said the Prince, "far away across the city I see a young man in a garret. He is leaning over a desk covered with papers, and in a tumbler by his side there is a bunch of withered violets. His hair is brown and crisp, and his lips are red as a pomegranate, and he has large and dreamy eyes. He is trying to finish a play for the Director of the Theatre, but he is too cold to write any more. There is no fire in the grate, and hunger has made him faint."

"I will wait with you one night longer," said the Swallow, who really had a good heart. "Shall I take him another ruby?"

"Alas! I have no ruby now," said the Prince; "my eyes are all that I have left. They are made of rare sapphires, which were brought out of India a thousand years ago. Pluck out one of them and take it to him. He will sell it to the jeweller, and buy food and firewood, and finish his play."

"Dear Prince," said the Swallow, "I cannot do that"; and he began to weep.

"Swallow, Swallow, little Swallow," said the Prince, "do as I command you."

So the Swallow plucked out the Prince's eye, and flew away to the student's garret. It was easy enough to get in, as there was a hole in the roof. Through this he darted, and came into the room. The young man had his head buried in his hands, so he did not hear the flutter of the bird's wings, and when he looked up he found the beautiful sapphire lying on the withered violets.

"I am beginning to be appreciated," he cried; "this is from some great admirer. Now I can finish my play," and he looked quite happy.

The next day the Swallow flew down to the harbour. He sat on the mast of a large vessel and watched the sailors hauling big chests out of the hold with ropes. "Heave a-hoy!" they shouted as each chest came up. "I am going to Egypt!" cried the Swallow, but nobody minded, and when the moon rose he flew back to the Happy Prince.

"I am come to bid you goodbye," he cried.

"Swallow, Swallow, little Swallow," said the Prince, "will you not stay with me one night longer?"

"It is winter," answered the Swallow, "and the chill snow will soon be here. In Egypt the sun is warm on the green palm-trees, and the crocodiles lie in the mud and look lazily about them. My companions are building a nest in the Temple of Baalbec, and the pink and white doves are watching them, and cooing to each other. Dear Prince, I must leave you, but I will never forget you, and next spring I will bring you back two beautiful jewels in place of those you have given away. The ruby shall be redder than a red rose, and the sapphire shall be as blue as the great sea."

"In the square below," said the Happy Prince, "there stands a little match-girl. She has let her matches fall in the gutter, and they are all spoiled. Her father will beat her if she does not bring home some money, and she is crying. She has no shoes or stockings, and her little head is bare. Pluck out my other eye, and give it to her, and her father will not beat her."

"I will stay with you one night longer," said the Swallow, "but I cannot pluck out your eye. You would be quite blind then."

"Swallow, Swallow, little Swallow," said the Prince, "do as I command you."

So he plucked out the Prince's other eye, and darted down with it. He swooped past the match-girl, and slipped the jewel into the palm of her hand. "What a lovely bit of glass," cried the little girl; and she ran home, laughing.

Then the Swallow came back to the Prince. "You are blind now," he said, "so I will stay with you always."

"No, little Swallow," said the poor Prince, "you must go away to Egypt."

"I will stay with you always," said the Swallow, and he slept at the Prince's feet.

All the next day he sat on the Prince's shoulder, and told him stories of what he had seen in strange lands. He told him of the red ibises, who stand in long rows on the banks of the Nile, and catch goldfish in their beaks; of the Sphinx, who is as old as the world itself, and lives in the desert, and knows everything; of the merchants, who walk slowly by the side of their camels and carry amber beads in their hands; of the King of the Mountains of the Moon, who is as black as ebony, and worships a large crystal; of the great green snake that sleeps in a palm-tree, and has twenty priests to feed it with honey-cakes; and of the pygmies who sail over a big lake on large flat leaves, and are always at war with the butterflies.

"Dear little Swallow," said the Prince, "you tell me of marvellous things, but more marvellous than anything is the suffering of men and of women. There is no Mystery so great as Misery. Fly over my city, little Swallow, and tell me what you see there."

So the Swallow flew over the great city, and saw the rich making merry in their beautiful houses, while the beggars were sitting at the gates. He flew into dark lanes, and saw the white faces of starving children looking out listlessly at the black streets. Under the archway of a bridge two little boys were lying in one another's arms to try and keep themselves warm. "How hungry we are!" they said. "You must not lie here," shouted the Watchman, and they wandered out into the rain.

Then he flew back and told the Prince what he had seen.

"I am covered with fine gold," said the Prince, "you must take it off, leaf by leaf, and give it to my poor; the living always think that gold can make them happy."

Leaf after leaf of the fine gold the Swallow picked off, till the Happy Prince looked quite dull and grey. Leaf after leaf of the fine gold he brought to the poor, and the children's faces grew rosier, and they laughed and played games in the street. "We have bread now!" they cried.

Then the snow came, and after the snow came the frost. The streets looked as if they were made of silver, they were so bright and glistening; long icicles like crystal daggers hung down from the eaves of the houses, everybody went about in furs, and the little boys wore scarlet caps and skated on the ice.

The poor little Swallow grew colder and colder, but he would not leave the Prince, he loved him too well. He picked up crumbs outside the baker's door when the baker was not looking, and tried to keep himself warm by flapping his wings.

But at last he knew that he was going to die. He had just strength to fly up to the Prince's shoulder once more. "Goodbye, dear Prince!" he murmured, "will you let me kiss your hand?"

"I am glad that you are going to Egypt at last, little Swallow," said the Prince, "you have stayed too long here; but you must kiss me on the lips, for I love you."

"It is not to Egypt that I am going," said the Swallow, "I am going to the House of Death. Death is the brother of Sleep, is he not?"

And he kissed the Happy Prince on the lips, and fell down dead at his feet.

At that moment a curious crack sounded inside the statue, as if something had broken. The fact is that the leaden heart had snapped right in two. It certainly was a dreadfully hard frost.

Early the next morning the Mayor was walking in the square below in company with the Town Councillors. As they passed the column he looked up at the statue: "Dear me! how shabby the Happy Prince looks!" he said.

"How shabby indeed!" cried the Town Councillors, who always agreed with the Mayor; and they went up to look at it.

"The ruby has fallen out of his sword, his eyes are gone, and he is golden no longer," said the Mayor; "in fact, he is little better than a beggar!"

"Little better than a beggar," said the Town Councillors.

"And here is actually a dead bird at his feet!" continued the Mayor. "We must really issue a proclamation that birds are not to be allowed to die here." And the Town Clerk made a note of the suggestion.

So they pulled down the statue of the Happy Prince. "As he is no longer beautiful he is no longer useful," said the Art Professor at the University.

Then they melted the statue in a furnace, and the Mayor held a meeting of the Corporation to decide what was to be done with the metal. "We must have another statue, of course," he said, "and it shall be a statue of myself."

"Of myself," said each of the Town Councillors, and they quarrelled. When I last heard of them they were quarrelling still.

"What a strange thing!" said the overseer of the workmen at the foundry. "This broken lead heart will not melt in the furnace. We must throw it away." So they threw it on a dust-heap where the dead Swallow was also lying.

"Bring me the two most precious things in the city," said God to one of His Angels; and the Angel brought Him the leaden heart and the dead bird.

"You have rightly chosen," said God, "for in my garden of Paradise this little bird shall sing for evermore, and in my city of gold the Happy Prince shall praise me."

KES

BARRY HINES

In the harsh urban world of northern industrial England, Billy finds an unexpected ally in life. Kes is the pride of his eye. When Billy sees her fly, he soars with her. He and his teacher, usually a remote figure of authority, are brought to a closer understanding of each other. For here the roles are reversed – Billy is doing the teaching.

THE HAWK WAS WAITING FOR HIM. As he unlocked the door she screamed and pressed her face to the bars. He selected the largest piece of beef, then, holding it firmly between finger and thumb with most of it concealed in his palm, he eased the door open and shoved his glove through the space. The hawk jumped on to his glove and attacked the meat. Billy swiftly followed his fist into the hut, secured the door behind him, and while the hawk was tearing at the fringe of beef, he attached her swivel and leash.

As soon as they got outside she looked up and tensed, feathers flat, eyes threatening. Billy stood still, whistling softly, waiting for her to relax and resume her feeding.

Then he walked round the back of the hut and held her high over his head as he climbed carefully over the fence. A tall hawthorn hedge bordered one side of the field, and the wind was strong and constant in the branches, but in the field it had been strained to a whisper. He reached the centre and unwound the leash from his glove, pulled it free of the swivel, then removed the swivel from the jesses and raised his fist. The hawk flapped her wings and fanned her tail, her claws still gripping the glove. Billy cast her off by nudging his glove upwards, and she banked away, completed a wide circuit then gained height rapidly, while he took the lure from his bag and unwound the line from the stick.

"Come on, Kes! Come on then!"

He whistled and swung the lure short-lined on a vertical plane. The hawk turned, saw it, and stooped . . .

"Casper!"

He glanced involuntarily across the field. Mr Farthing was climbing the fence and waving to him. The hawk grabbed the lure and Billy allowed her to take it to the ground.

"Bloody hell fire."

He pegged the stick into the soil and stood up. Mr Farthing was tiptoeing towards him, concentrating on his passage through the grass. With his overcoat on, and his trousers pinched up, he looked like a day-tripper paddling at the seaside. Billy allowed him to get within thirty yards, then stopped him by raising one hand.

"You'll have to stop there, Sir."

"I hope I'm not too late."

"No, Sir, but you'll have to watch from there."

"That's all right. If you think I'm too near I can go back to the fence."

"No, you'll be all right there, as long as you stand still."

"I won't breathe."

He smiled and put his hands in his overcoat pockets. Billy crouched down and made in towards the hawk along the lure line. He offered her a scrap of beef, and she stepped off the lure on to his glove. He allowed her to take the beef, then he stood up and cast her off again. She wheeled away, high round the field. Billy plucked the stick from the ground and began to swing the lure. The hawk turned and stooped at it. Billy watched her as she descended, waiting for the right moment as she accelerated rapidly towards him. Now. He straightened his arm and lengthened the line, throwing the lure into her path and sweeping it before her in a downward arc, then twitching it up too steep for her attack, making her throw up, her impetus carrying her high into the air. She turned and stooped again. Billy presented the lure again. And again. Each time smoothly before her, an inch before her so that the next wing-beat must catch it, or the next. Working the lure like a top matador his cape. Encouraging the hawk, making her stoop faster and harder, making Mr Farthing hold his breath at each stoop and near miss. Each time she made off Billy called her continually, then stopped in concentration as he timed his throw and leaned into the long drawing of the lure and the hawk in its wake, her eyes fixed, beak open, angling her body and adjusting her flight to any slight shift in speed or direction.

She tried a new tactic, and came in low, seeming to flit within a pocket of silence close to the ground. Billy flexed at the knees and flattened the plane of the swing, allowing the lengthening line to pay out before her.

"Come on, this time, Kes! This time!"

She shortened her stoop, and counter stoop, which increased the frequency of her attacks, and made Billy pivot, and whirl, and watch, but never lose control of the lure or its pursuer. Until finally the hawk sheered away

and began to ring up high over the hawthorn hedge.

"Come on then, Kes! Once more! Last time!"

And she came, head first, wings closed, swooping down, hurtling down towards Billy, who waited, then lured her – WHOOSH – up, throwing up, ringing up, turning; and as she stooped again Billy twirled the lure and threw it high into her path. She caught it, and clutched it down to the ground.

He allowed her to take the remaining beef scrap from the lure, then took her up and attached the swivel and leash. She looked up sharply at a series of claps. Mr Farthing was applauding softly. Billy started towards him and they met half-way, the hawk fixing the stranger every second of their approach.

"Marvellous, Casper! Brilliant! That's one of the most exciting things I've ever seen!"

Billy blushed, and there was silence while they both looked at the hawk. The hawk looked back, her breast still heaving from her exertions.

"It's beautiful, isn't it? Do you know, this is the first time I've ever been really close to a hawk?"

He raised a hand towards it. The hawk pecked and clawed at it. He withdrew his hand quickly.

"Goodness! . . . It's not very friendly, is it?"

Billy smiled and stroked her breast, ruttling under her wings with his fingers.

"Seems all right with you though."

"Only 'cos she thinks I'm not bothered."

"What do you mean?"

"Well when she used to peck me I kept my finger there as though it didn't hurt. So after a bit she just packed it in."

"That's good. I'd never have thought of that."

"You'll notice I always keep my hands away from her claws though. You don't get used to them striking you."

Mr Farthing looked at the yellow scaled shins, the four spanned toes, the steely claws gripping the gauntlet.

"No, I'll bet you don't."

Billy produced the sparrow from his bag and pushed it up between the finger and thumb of his glove. The hawk immediately pinned it with one foot and with her beak began to pluck the feathers from its head. Plucking and tossing in bunches, left and right, sowing them to the wind. Baring a spot, then a patch of puckered pink skin. She nipped this skin and pulled, ripping a hole in it and revealing the pale shine of the skull, as fragile and delicately curved as one of the sparrow's own eggs. Scrunch. The shell crumpled, and the whole crown was torn away and swallowed at one gulp. Another bite and the head was gone; even the beak was swallowed, being first finely crushed into fragments. Billy eased the sparrow up between his fingers, revealing most of its body. The hawk lowered her head and began to pluck the breast and wings. The breast fluff puffed away like fairy clocks; the wing quills twirled to the ground like ash keys. Occasionally the hawk shook her head, trying to dislodge feathers which had stuck to the blood on her beak. If this failed she scratched at them with her claws, the flickering points passing within fractions of her eyes, wincing as though half in enjoyment, half in pain, like someone having a good scratch at a nettle rash.

She cleared most of the breast, then pierced the skin with her beak and tore it open, exposing beneath the wafer of breast meat the minute organs, coiled and compact, packed perfectly into the tiny frame. The hawk disturbed their composition by reaching inside and dragging the intestines out. They swung from her beak, with the stomach attached like a watch on a chain. Then she snuffled and gobbled them down in a slithering putty-coloured pile.

"Uh!"

"Full o' vitamins them, Sir."

The liver, a purply-brown pad; the heart, a slippery pebble; leaving only the carcass, a mess of skin and bone and feathers, which the hawk pulled apart and devoured in pieces. Any bones which were too big to crush and swallow comfortably were flicked away; clean white fragments, precise miniatures, knobbled and hollowed and lost in the grass. Until only the legs remained. The hawk nibbled delicately at the thighs, stripping them of their last shred of meat, leaving only the tarsi and the feet, which she spat aside. All gone. She stood up and shook her head.

Mr Farthing followed Billy over the fence, round to the front of the shed, and watched through the bars while the hawk was being released inside. She flew straight to her perch, lowered her head and began to feake, using the wood as a strop for her beak. Then she stood up and roused herself. Billy opened the door and stepped aside for Mr Farthing to enter. He squeezed quickly inside and they stood side by side looking at the hawk, which had settled down on one foot, her other foot bunched up in her feathers.

"Keep lookin' away from her, Sir, they don't like being stared at, hawks."

"Right."

Mr Farthing glanced round at the whitewashed walls and ceiling, the fresh mutes on the clean shelves, the clean dry sand on the floor.

"You keep it nice and clean in here."

"You have to. There's less chance of her gettin' sick then."

"You think a lot about that bird, don't you?"

Billy looked up at him, all the way up to his eyes.

"Course I do. Wouldn't you if it wa' yours?"

Mr Farthing laughed quietly, once.

"Yes I suppose I would. You like wildlife, don't you, Billy?"

"Yes, Sir."

"Have you ever kept any more birds before this one?"

"Stacks. Animals an' all. I had a young fox cub once, reared it and let it go. It wa' a little blinder."

"What birds have you kept?"

"All sorts, maggies, jackdaws; I had a young jay once; that wa' murder though, they're right hard to feed, an' it nearly died. I wouldn't have one again, they're best left to their mothers."

"And which has been your favourite?"

Billy looked at Mr Farthing as though his mentality had suddenly deteriorated to that of an idiot.

"You what, Sir?"

"You mean the hawk?"

"T'others weren't in t'same street."

"Why not? What's so special about this one?"

Billy bent down and scooped up a fistful of sand.

"I don't know right. It just is that's all."

"What about magpies? They're handsome birds. And jays, they've got beautiful colours."

"It's not only t'colours though, that's nowt."

"What is it then?"

Billy allowed a trickle of sand out of his fist on to his left pump. The grains bounced off the rubber toe cap like a column of tap water exploding in the sink. He shook his head and shrugged his shoulder. Mr Farthing stepped forward and raised one hand.

"What I like about it is its shape; it's so beautifully proportioned. The neat head, the way the wings fold over on its back. Its tail, just the right length, and that down on the thighs, just like a pair of plus-fours."

He modelled the hawk in the air, emphasizing each point of description with corresponding sweeps and curves of his hands.

"It's the sort of thing you want to paint, or model in clay. Painting would be best I should think, you'd be able to get all those lovely brown markings in then."

"It's when it's flying though, Sir, that's when it's got it over other birds, that's when it's at its best."

"Yes I agree with you. Do you know, you can tell it's a good flyer just by looking at it sitting there."

"It's 'cos it looks streamlined."

"It's what I was saying about proportion, I think that's got something to do with it. There's a saying about racehorses that if they look good, they probably are good. I think the same applies here."

"It does."

"And yet there's something weird about it when it's flying."

"You what, Sir?" Hawks are t'best flyers there are."

"I don't mean . . ."

"I'm not sayin' there isn't other good uns; look at swallows an' swifts, an' peewits when they're tumblin' about in t'air. An' there's gulls an' all. I used to watch 'em for hours when we used to go away. It wa' t'best at Scarborough, where you could get on t'cliff top an' watch 'em. They're still not t'same though. Not to me anyroad."

"I don't mean anything to do with the beauty of its flight, that's marvellous. I mean . . . well, when it flies there's something about it that makes you feel strange."

"I think I know what you mean, Sir, you mean everything seems to go dead quiet."

"That's it!"

His exclamation made the hawk jerk up and tense.

"Steady on, Sir, you'll frighten her to death."

Mr Farthing pointed two fingers at his temple and triggered his thumb.

"Sorry, I forgot."

The hawk roused and settled again.

"It was just that you got it so right about the silence."

"Other folks have noticed that an' all. I know a farmer, an' he says it's the same wi' owls. He says that he's seen 'em catchin' mice in his yard at night, an' that when they swoop down, you feel like poking your ears to make 'em pop because it goes that quiet."

"Yes, that's right. That's how I felt, it's as though it was flying in a, . . . in a, . . . in a pocket of silence, that's it, a pocket of silence. That's strange, isn't it?"

"They're strange birds."

"And this feeling, this silence, it must carry over. Have you noticed how quietly we're speaking? And how strange it sounded when I raised my voice. It was almost like shouting in a church."

"It's 'cos they're nervous, Sir. You have to keep your voice down."

"No, it's more than that. It's instinctive. It's a kind of respect."

"I know, Sir. That's why it makes me mad when I take her out and I'll hear somebody say, 'Look there's Billy Casper there wi' his pet hawk.' I could shout at 'em; it's not a pet, Sir, hawks are not pets. Or when folks stop me and say, 'Is it tame?' Is it heck tame, it's trained that's all. It's fierce, an' it's wild, an' it's not bothered about anybody, not even about me right. And that's why it's great."

"A lot of people wouldn't understand that sentiment though, they like pets they can make friends with; make a fuss of, cuddle a bit, boss a bit; don't you agree?"

"Ye', I suppose so. I'm not bothered about that though. I'd sooner have her, just to look at her, an' fly her. That's enough for me. They can keep their rabbits an' their cats an' their talkin' budgies, they're rubbish compared wi' her."

Mr Farthing glanced down at Billy, who was staring at the hawk, breathing rapidly.

"Yes, I think you're right; they probably are."

"Do you know, Sir, I feel as though she's doing me a favour just lettin' me stand here."

"Yes I know what you mean. It's funny though, when you try to analyse it, exactly what it is about it. For example, it's not its size is it?"

"No, Sir."

"And it doesn't look terribly fearsome; in fact there are moments when it looks positively babyish. So what is it then?"

"I don't know."

Mr Farthing moulded a fender of sand with the toe of one shoe, then slowly looked up at the hawk.

"I think it's a kind of pride, and as you say independence. It's like an awareness, a satisfaction with its own beauty and prowess. It seems to look you straight in the eye and say, 'Who the hell are you anyway?' It reminds me of that poem by Lawrence, 'If men were as much men as lizards are lizards they'd be worth looking at.' It just seems proud to be itself."

"Yes, Sir."

They stood silent for a minute, then Mr Farthing pushed his overcoat and jacket sleeves up to look at the time. The watch face was concealed under his shirt cuff. He revealed the face by lifting the cuff and sliding the strap down his wrist.

"Good lord! Look at the time, it's twenty past one. We'd better be off."

He fumbled for the door fastener and backed out of the shed.

"I'll give you a lift if you like. I'm here in the car."

Billy blushed and shook his head. Mr Farthing smiled in at him through the bars.

"What's the matter, wouldn't do your reputation any good to be seen travelling with a teacher?"

"It's not that, Sir . . . I've one or two things to do first."

"Please yourself then. But you're going to have to look sharp, or you'll be late."

"I know, I'll not be long."

"Right. I'll be off then."

His face disappeared from the bars, and reappeared a few seconds later.

"And thanks for the display, I really enjoyed it. You're an expert lad."

His face disappeared again, and for a few moments his barred charcoal back blocked the whole square. Then light, and other shapes like jigsaw pieces, grew round his receding silhouette, the house, the garage, the garden.

A car engine bleated. Bleated again and caught. BRUM-BRUMMED to a climax, then hummed away on a rising pitch.

Billy looked down and began to guide an oblong furry pellet through the sand with one toe. There was a kink in the fading car sound, a pause like a missed heartbeat as it changed up to a softer tone, and the final fade.

Billy picked the pellet up and inspected it in his palm. It was the size of a blackbird's egg, charcoal coloured, and shining faintly as though lacquered. He rolled it around his hand awhile, sniffed it, then carefully crumbled it with his fingertips. Inside the lacquered crust the fur was a lighter shade of grey, snuff dry, and wrapped inside the fur were tiny bones, and a tiny skull, with sets of dot-sized teeth dotted to its tiny jaws. Billy rubbed the fur to ash, and gently blew it away like chaff from grain, leaving only the bones and skull in his palm. He placed the skull on the shelf behind the door, then began to push the bones around with his forefinger; aimlessly at first, then linking them into a triangle, which he immediately destroyed, and reformed as an angular C. He studied this letter, then tried to remould it, but he could only make a D, so he shuffled the bones until their formation was meaningless.

Selecting the longest bone, he pincered it, pin thin, between his forefinger and thumb. The pressure drained two small patches of his skin white; then the points punctured, and a spot of blood formed on his fingertip; followed by a second on his thumb. He frowned and squeezed. This made him close one eye and bite his lips. The bone remained intact. Billy opened the pincers, and it stuck up out of the skin of his thumb like a little standard. He turned his thumb over, nail upwards. The bone still stuck, so he pulled it out and snapped it. The crack made the hawk open its eyes. Billy dropped the bones and carefully ground them into the sand with his pumps. Only the skull remained. He turned it to face the bars, then quietly left the hut, locked up, and with a final glance at the hawk, walked away up the path.

THE WEDGE-TAILED EAGLE

GEOFFREY DUTTON

The collision between man and the natural world, brought about by man's madness, man's vanity, is perfectly illustrated here.

THROUGH THE HOT, cloudless days in the back of New South Wales, there is always something beside the sun watching you from the sky. Over the line of the hills, or above the long stretches of plains, a black dot swings round and round; and its circles rise slowly or fall slowly, or simply remain at the same height, swinging in endless indolent curves, while the eyes watch the miles of earth below, and the six- or maybe nine-foot wingspan remains motionless in the air. You know that there is nothing you can do which will not be observed, that the circling eagle, however small the distance may make it, however aloof its flight may seem, has always fixed upon the earth an attention as fierce as its claws.

But the eagles watch the sky as well as the earth, and not only for other birds; when an Air Force Station was established in their country in 1941, they were not alarmed by the noisy yellow aeroplanes. Occasionally they would even float in circles across the aerodrome itself, and then disappear again behind the hills; the pilots had little fear of colliding with one of these circling, watchful birds. The vast, brown-black shape of the eagle would appear before the little Tiger Moth biplane and then be gone. There was nothing more to it. No question of haste or flapping of wings, simply a flick over and down and then the eagle would resume its circling. Sometimes a pilot would chase the bird and would find, unexpectedly, no response; the eagle would seem not to notice the aeroplane and hold the course of its circling until the very moment when collision seemed inevitable. Then there would be the quick turn over, under, or away from the plane, with the great span of wings unstirred. The delay and the quick manoeuvre would be done with a princely detachment and consciousness of superiority, the eagle in the silence of its wings scorning the roar and fuss of the aircraft and its engine.

Two pilots from the station were drinking one day in the local town with one of the farmers over whose land they used to fly.

"Two of us, you know, could do it," one of them said. "By yourself it's hopeless. The eagle can outfly you without moving his wings. But with two of you, one could chase him round while the other climbed above and dived at him. That way you'd at least get him flustered."

The farmer was not at all hopeful.

"Maybe it'd take more than a couple of planes to fluster an eaglehawk. There's a big one around my place, just about twelve feet across. I wish you could get him. Though if you did hit him, there mightn't be much left of your little aeroplane."

"It always beats me why you call them eaglehawks," said one of the pilots. "The wedge-tailed eagle is the biggest eagle in the world. You ought to pay him more respect, the most magnificent, majestic bird there is."

The farmer was hostile to this idea of majesty.

"Have you ever seen them close-up? Or ever seen them feeding? The king of birds landing on a lolly-legged lamb and tearing him to bits. Or an old, dead, fly-blown ewe that's been fool enough to lie down with her legs uphill. Watch him hacking his way into their guts, with the vermin dancing all over his stinking brown feathers. Then all you've got to do is to let him see you five hundred yards off and up he flaps, slow and awkward, to a myall where he sits all bunched-up looking as if he's going to overbalance the little tree. Still, go ahead with your scheme. I'd like to see you beat one at his own game."

He left, and the two others continued discussing their plans. A pilot in a small, aerobatic aircraft is like a child. He longs for something to play with. He can be happy enough, rolling and looping by himself in the sky, but happiness changes to a kind of ecstasy when there is someone against whom to match his skill, or someone to applaud him when he low-flies through the unforeseeable complications of tree and rock, hill and river. The contest becomes more wonderful the nearer it approaches death, when all else is forgotten in the concentration of the minute. The pilot who fights with bullets and shells is ecstatically involved in his action. This fight with the wedge-tailed eagle was to be to the death, not a battle of bullets or shells, but of skill against inborn mastery. The risk of death would be there, just the same, both for the bird and for the pilot supported by the fragile wood and fabric of the aeroplane.

One cloudless morning the pilots flew off together, in close formation, towards the valley of the farmer's house. The sky was as clean as a gun-barrel and the sun hit them both in the back of the neck as they flew westward towards the scrubby range and the valley beyond. The pilot of the leading aircraft loosened his helmet and let the wind, like a cool rushing sense of elation and freedom, blow around his neck and hair. Like the eagle, he was a watcher, one from whom no secrets could hide on the earth below. The country matched the element in which he moved: both hard and unforgiving of mistakes, yet endlessly stretching, magnificent in freedom. Neither the air nor this land would bring anything for the asking; but they would offer all manner of their peculiar riches to anyone who could conquer them by work and vigilance and love. The foolish and the weak perished like the sheep stuck in the wet mud of the drying dams, in sight of water for the lack of which they died.

As he approached the hills, the earth below him and the creeks were brown and dry as a walnut, with a strip of green along the river and a few bright squares where a farmer had sunk a bore and put in a few acres of lucerne. A mob of sheep stirred along in a cloud of dust through a few scattered myalls and gum trees. He finally bounced over the hills through air rough from the hot rocks, and turning away from the other aeroplane, moved up the broad valley, searching the sky for the black dot of an eagle wheeling and wheeling like a windmill on its side. There was no sign of anything, not even of a cloud or a high whirly of dust, which in an empty sky looks like a patch of rust in a gun-barrel. Everything seemed to him shiny and empty, yet somehow waiting to go off.

He made a long leisurely run up the valley, a few feet above the ground, lifting his wing over a fence or two, turning round a gum tree or away from a mob of sheep. The only other sign of life was the farmer standing near his truck by the gate of a paddock. He answered his wave, turned and flew over him, and then continued up the valley. Above him, in the other aeroplane, his friend waited for something to happen.

He ran his wheels almost along the ground and turned another fence. Suddenly the whole top of a tree flapped off in front of him and the eagle disappeared behind him before he could turn. Another bird rose from a dead sheep a few hundred yards away, but the pilot's whole attention was concentrated on the bird that had risen from the myall tree. It was undoubtedly the big eagle of which the farmer had told them.

By the time he had turned and come back in a climb the eagle was five hundred feet above him. He opened the throttle wide and pulled the strap of his helmet tight. He looked for the other plane and saw that his friend was moving towards them and climbing also, so that with the added height he could dive as they had planned.

The pilot was astonished to find that he was being out-climbed without the bird even moving a feather of its wings. On the hot, unseen currents it swung lazily round and round, its motionless wings always above the quivering, roaring aircraft. To make things worse, the pilot, in order to climb as quickly as possible, had to move in a straight line and then turn back, whereas the eagle sailed up in a close spiral. His hand pushed harder on the small knob of the throttle already wide open against the stop. Perhaps the battle would come to no more than this, the noisy pursuit of an enemy who could never be reached.

Yet the eagle, its mastery already established, now deliberately ceased climbing and waited for the aeroplane to struggle up to its level. The pilot, wondering if the farmer below had seen his humiliation, pressed on above the bird, where at about three thousand feet he levelled off and waved to his friend above that the battle was about to begin.

He came round in a curve at the bird, the aeroplane on the edge of stalling, juddering all over, the control-stick suddenly going limp in his hand as a pump-handle when a tank is dry, the slots on the end of the wings clattering above him; and then, just as he ducked his head to avoid the shining curved beak, the braced black and brown feathers, the sky amazingly was empty in front of him. The eagle had flicked over as lightly as a swallow, with no sign of panic or haste. He looked over and saw it below him, circling as quietly as if nothing in the whole morning, in the sky or on the land, had disturbed its watchful mastery of the air.

As the pilot dived towards it and followed it around again, he saw his friend drop his wing and come down, steep and straight, to make the attack they had planned. He could see that the eagle, under its apparent negligence, was watching him and not the diving plane. This was the moment for which they had waited, when the eagle would break away as usual, but to find another aeroplane coming at it before it had time to move. The pilot's heart lunged inside him like the needle of the revolution counter on the instrument panel. Waiting until his friend had only another few hundred feet of his dive left, he jerked the controls hard over towards the shining feathers of the bird. It turned and fell below him, exactly as they had hoped it would. The pilot pulled himself up against his straps to watch its flight. The other aeroplane was on it just as it began its circling again. But the collision did not happen. The plane shot on and began to pull up out of its dive; the eagle recovered again into its slow swinging, a few hundred feet lower.

Yet it had shown a little concern. For the first time a fraction of dignity had been lost: momentarily the great wings had been disturbed a little from their full stretch. It had been startled into a quick defensive action. The pilot's excitement now blotted out everything but the battle in progress, leaving him poised between earth and sky, forgetful of both except as a blur of blue, a rush of brown. The last thing he saw on land had been the farmer's truck coming across the paddocks to a point somewhere below. Then all the vanity and pride in him had responded to the fact that there was someone to watch him. Now, no response existed except to the detail of the black, polished brownness of the eagle's plumage, the glistening beak, the wedge-shaped tail. His excitement was at that intensity which is part of hope, his first sight of achievement. Previously, the insolent negligence of the bird had destroyed his confidence, and had almost made the air feel the alien element it really was. In contrast with all his noisy manoeuvring, his juggling with engine and controls, the eagle had scorned him with its silence, with its refusal to flap its wings, its mastery of the motionless sweep, the quick flick to safety and then the motionless circling again. The pilot had begun to wonder who was playing with whom. Perhaps the bird would suddenly turn, dive, rip him with a talon, and slide sideways down the vast slope to earth.

Yet now the eagle had been forced to move its wings, and he had seen the first sign of victory. Sweat poured round his helmet and down his neck and chest. His shirt clung wetly first to his flesh and then to the parachute harness. He looked at his altimeter and saw that they were down to seven hundred feet. Above him his friend was ready.

He turned in again towards the eagle. The aeroplane shivered and clung to height, on the last fraction of speed before the spin. Feeling the stiffness of his hands and feet on the controls, he told himself to relax like the eagle in front of him. He looked quickly upwards and saw his

K217

friend begin to dive. This was the second stage of their plan. The eagle, however little sign of it appeared, knew now that both aeroplanes were attacking. It circled, still on unmoving wings, but subtler and harder to follow, and shifted height slightly as it swung around.

The other plane was almost past him in its dive when he completed his turn in a vicious swing towards the eagle; he missed, spun, corrected, looked up to see the other aeroplane, which had dived this time far below the eagle, coming almost vertically up below the just-levelled bird.

The eagle heard and saw, and flicked over to where, before, safety had always been emptily waiting for it. It flashed, wings still gloriously outstretched, straight into the right-hand end of the upper mainplane of the aircraft, exactly where the metal slot curves across the wood and fabric. Its right wing, at the point where the hard, long feathers give way to the soft, curved feathers of the body, snapped away and fluttered down to earth. The left wing folded into the body, stretched and folded again, as the heavy box of bone, beak and claw plunged and slewed to the ground. The pilot could not watch the last few feet of its descent. For the first time he was grateful to the roar of the motor that obscured the thud of the body striking earth.

The two pilots landed in the paddock, and, leaving the engines running, walked over to the dark mass of feathers. One of them turned off to the side and came back holding the severed wing. It was almost as big as the man himself.

The two of them stood in silence. The moment of skill and danger was past, and the dead body before them proclaimed their victory. Frowning with the glare of the sun and the misery of their achievement they both looked down at the piteous, one-winged eagle. Not a mark of blood was on it, the beak glistening and uncrushed, the ribbed feet and talons clenched together. It was not the fact of death that kept them in silence; the watcher could not always keep his station in the air. What both of them could still see was the one-winged heap of bone and feathers, slewing and jerking uncontrolled to earth.

In the distance they heard the noise of the farmer's truck approaching, and saw it stop at a gate and the farmer wave as he got out to open it. They quickly picked up the bird and its wing, and ran with them to the little hillock covered in rocks at the corner of the paddock. Between two large rocks they folded both wings across the bird and piled stones above it; and then, each lifting, carried a large flat stone and placed it above the others.

As they ran back towards the aeroplanes a black dot broke from the hills and swung out above them, circling round and round, watching the truck accelerate and then stop as the two aeroplanes turned, taxied and slid into the air before it could reach them.

GODHANGER

DICK KING-SMITH

The wild birds of Godhanger Wood against the gamekeeper and his gun. An uneven contest, until the Skymaster (or is it God?) takes a hand. A tale of birds, yes, but a tale too of good and evil, a timeless tale.

THREE HUNDRED METRES BELOW, Godhanger Wood lay still in evening sunshine. Gliding silently across the darkening sky, his flight feathers spread like fingertips, Loftus the raven looked down at the massed treetops, the green of their myriad leaves now changing to the reds, golds and browns of autumn.

The shape of the wood was plain to him, lying along the slope of a valley or combe. In outline it resembled the head and neck of a horse. There was even a clearing at just the place to give an impression of an eye.

In the shelter of the hill, the hardwood trees – oak, beech, ash, sycamore and chestnut – grew for the most part straight and skyward, but at the ridge, along the horse's neck, only a hog-mane of thorn and hedge-maple survived, bent crookback by the fierce sea-winds.

The breeze on which Loftus rode came also from the west, a light air, a breath only, and his all-seeing eyes marked how motionless was the canopy of Godhanger Wood. The only movement below him was that of another bird, almost as large as himself but dark brown instead of his glossy sable, that wheeled endlessly above the valley bottom on broad unmoving wings. Buzzard-baiting appealed to Loftus' sense of humour, and he tipped off his pitch and fell like a black arrow towards the big hawk.

"Whee-oo!" cried the bird in distress at the sound of the raven's coming, and threw himself sideways in frantic flapping haste. Again, "Whee-oo!" mewed the buzzard, as Loftus shot past him, and his plaintive cries were echoed by his mate, hunting behind the hill.

"Pee-oo! Pee-oo!" called the hen bird in reply, and they said to each other, "It's that damned raven again." "I suppose he thinks it's amusing."

At that moment they saw Loftus come swooping up over the top of the hill, and, still complaining, they made their heavy way off in search of more peaceful hunting grounds.

Chuckling in his deep voice, the raven climbed above the wood, circling as he gained height, and watching the treetops darkening as the daylight died.

Now his old familiar nesting-place beckoned, high on a sheltered ledge on the Atlantic cliffs, with his old familiar mate, mother in her time to his many children; the gruff-spoken, hairy-chinned, comfortable roosting partner at the end of so many thousands of days. He was just about to turn for home when he saw a solitary black and white bird flying silently along the wood's edge. As he watched, it perched for a moment in the top of a single outlying skeleton-elm, long tail dipping up and down, and then flew suddenly and rapidly away with loud calls of alarm.

"Chakka-chakka-chakka-chak!" cried Myles the magpie,

and Loftus circled higher still. He knew Myles for a thief and a double-dyed villain, but he also knew better than to doubt the 'pie's warning.

And at that precise moment the evening's peace was shattered by the blast of a gunshot. After a heartbeat's pause came the noise of a second shot, followed by a thin agonized screaming that ceased as suddenly as it had arisen. Silence fell again on Godhanger Wood as the raven beat away towards the west.

The two spent cartridges spun away as the gamekeeper broke open his gun. He reloaded and stood still, eyes narrowed, watching his dog working a bramble-patch. Very soon she came running to the man, a squealing rabbit in her mouth, and laid it, broken-legged and bulging-eyed, before him. The noise stopped abruptly as the gamekeeper took the rabbit and broke its neck.

One glance at the limp body told him that it was a milky doe, its belly plucked of the soft fur in which now, somewhere, its kittens were warmly snuggled and would soon lie cold and stiff.

Gun in the crook of his left arm, he pulled from his right-hand coat pocket a bone-handled knife and opened its ten-centimetre blade. Neatly he slashed the middle of the doe's upturned belly between the two rows of swollen teats, closed and replaced the knife, then reached in and twisted out guts and paunch, which he tossed away into the undergrowth.

The dog made no move but sat watching, hoping, on this occasion rightly, that the carcase would be hers at the end of the day. The gamekeeper slipped the rabbit into his game-bag and wiped his red hand on the silky hair of the spaniel's back. Then he straightened up and set off again, dog at heel, with long strides through the tall trees of Godhanger.

All was quiet as before his coming, all was as it had been, save for two orange-coloured cartridge cases on the ground, and, caught upon a bramble, a little festoon of warm innards whose coils still wriggled and slid uneasily.

A meat-fly landed upon the guts, and stood, moving its feet in pleased anticipation until it was dislodged by a final spasmodic motion of the glazing intestines. They slipped from the briar and fell to the ground.

After a gap of time the stillness of the darkening wood was broken. At intervals, among the great oaks and beeches, there were a few small stands of larches, and into these, homecoming pigeons began to crash. Nearer, a pair of little owls started up their shrill, plaintive cries. Above the bramble-patch, on a low bough of a big horse chestnut, a robin sang with that heart-catching wistfulness that tells of summer gone and hard cold nights to come. The breeze had dropped to nothing. Nothing moved.

Suddenly, quite silently, a head appeared, poking out beneath the tangle of blackberry bushes. It was a blackish head with white marks about the sharp muzzle and between eye and ear.

For a moment the head moved to and fro, quick, questing nostrils dilated to suck in the gut-scent – and then, out of the briar patch slid the low, dark, humpbacked shape of Rippin the polecat, foul-smelling killer of any creature that might come his way. Unlike other animals, it was the nature of his kind to kill and keep on killing. He was programmed to do so. Mice, rats, ground-nesting birds, frogs, snakes – all were fair game to Rippin, as indeed was far larger prey when chance offered: in his time he had put paid to many chickens, and once, one glorious, never-to-be-forgotten winter's night, sixteen turkeys had died to satisfy his blood-lust. Such monsters, of course, he had not been able to drag away, but they had provided a feast of his favourite delicacy: the brains.

However, Rippin was not fussy. Rabbit guts would do for starters. He had begun to tug and gulp at them, growling softly in his throat, when suddenly, from out of nowhere, a broad-winged shape came swooping noiselessly upon him with talons hanging ready to grasp, only to sheer away at the last moment as the polecat rose up on his hind legs to his full height, all forty-five centimetres of it, his mouth agape, his coarse fur on end, and chattered in fearless fury.

"Damn you! Damn you!" he raved, dancing in his rage. "If I could only catch hold of you, I'd have the feathers off you, I'd tear your throat out, suck your blood, chew up your great staring eyeballs, I'd kill you, kill you, kill you!" And the air about grew thick with his choking, acrid stink.

Circling, the tawny owl flew back and pitched on a branch of the chestnut to stare silently down, till at last the polecat ceased his cursing and made off, towing a rope of guts with him and grumbling all the while. "Bloody owls, I hate 'em, I hate 'em," the bird could hear, until finally the sound passed beyond even his acute earshot.

"Horrible beast," said the tawny owl softly to himself. He straightened a feather or two on his streaky breast, and swivelled his round head to look all about him.

"That's the nastiest-natured creature in Godhanger, bar none," he said. "Sure as my name is Glyde."

"Glyde."

The word was instantly repeated, like an echo. But it was not an echo. The name was spoken in a different voice, a voice whose authority was instantly recognizable, even in the uttering of that monosyllable.

Glyde looked up into the branches high above. "Master?" he said. "Is it you?"

From somewhere high within the still-leafy crown of the

horse chestnut, a great shape dropped on silent wings, and pitched upon the tawny owl's branch, almost half a metre below him. Even so, their heads were on a level. This was the mighty bird who had come to Godhanger Wood, known to those that lived there as the Skymaster.

Some of the birds of the wood had come together as followers of the Skymaster, and all these carried different pictures of him in their minds. Because all found themselves unable to meet his gaze directly, each tended to think of him in the image of his own kind, as some sort of hawk or falcon or crow or owl. Only once in their lives were they able to look directly at him, and then it was too late.

Glyde looked away as usual, saying, "You called, Master?"

Had he been able to see the other's eyes, he would have noticed a twinkle in them. "'The nastiest-natured creature in Godhanger' I think you remarked?" said the Skymaster. His tone was not of rebuke but of amusement. "Why so, my friend?"

"He is evil-tempered," said Glyde.

"He was angry, yes, certainly. But there are times when anger rouses each and every one of us."

"Not you, Master."

"That you have not known me angered does not mean, Glyde, that I have never been so, or that you will never so see me. Anger may be healthy, cleansing, a relief to the spirit at certain times, just as a violent thunderstorm clears the air and cools the overheated land."

The tawny owl scratched the side of his round face with a claw. "At certain times, maybe," he said reasonably. "But Rippin the foumart is always angry." He used the old name for a polecat, the marten that is foul-scented, though the word itself was meaningless to him, since like almost all the birds, he had little or no sense of smell.

"And," he went on, "he is always hungry for the taste of blood."

"Do you not kill?" asked the Skymaster.

"Yes, but for food, not for fun, Master. To feed myself, my mate, our owlets. To this end the roosting bird must die, the rat, the mouse, the cockchafer. I cannot live by berries alone. It is not in my nature."

"Yet your nature – for this is what you are saying – is less nasty than the polecat's? You are a nicer creature (remembering that just now it was you who dived upon him), you are more to be esteemed, of greater value, more likeable?"

"Yes, Master," said Glyde stubbornly. "I think I am."

"Perhaps then," said the Skymaster, "you had better try to think better of Rippin the polecat, lest you too become nasty-natured, as you say he is," and he spread his great wings and sailed away into the darkness.

The tawny owl sat for some minutes and bent his head to peer at the ground below. The moonlight glinted upon the brass ends of two cartridge cases that lay in the short grass of the floor of the wood, and Glyde put his head on one side to consider better this unusual pair of shining eyes.

His was not the only curious gaze, for in a moment there came the tiniest scratching noise to tense his muscles, and a woodmouse appeared from its hole between the tree roots and began a series of little darting runs towards the strange objects. Instantly Glyde dropped like a stone from his branch to take the mouse in one foot. The four curved talons crushed out its life, and into Glyde's beak it went headfirst, the tail sticking out just for a second, waving a little as though the woodmouse were still alive.

Then from deeper in the wood there came the noise of grunting, and the tawny owl gulped down his meal and flew silently away.

Now the grunting sounds grew louder, and presently there emerged into a moonlit clearing a low, heavy animal that walked flat-footed with the slow rolling shuffle of a bear, stopping often for a scratch or to nose about for food.

Baldwin the badger was the least fussy of feeders. Anything that was edible he ate – fledgling birds fallen from the nest, mice, voles, hedgehogs even, plus insects, especially the larvae of wasp and bumble-bee, and quantities of earthworms.

"Snakes," he would say, "are very tasty. I'm very partial to a nice grass-snake. But what I really relish is a nest of young rabbits. Delicious, they are."

Never a fast mover, even as a young boar, Baldwin in old age took life very steadily. Let the junior badgers go galloping about Godhanger, burning up their energy in play, or mating, or fighting. He was past all that, he told himself. A solitary badger now, he told himself everything, finding comfort in this, as the old often do.

"Always look after Number One, Baldwin, my boy," he would say. "You're not so sprack as you were, and the old bones ache a bit when the wind's in the north. So long as you can keep the old belly full, that's what matters. Still got your teeth, praise be. And your nose."

Now, as Baldwin reached the bramble-patch beneath the horse chestnut, that nose brought him a sudden clear message.

"Hello, hello!" he said. "I smell rabbit," and he poked his white-striped head into the undergrowth and sniffed deeply.

The doe whose guts Rippin had eaten had been a stub-rabbit, a rabbit that contrives to live its life not in tunnels

below ground but in runs beneath heather or furze bushes or, as here, within a tangle of briars.

Nothing had remained of the doe but her pelt, flung on the midden behind the gamekeeper's cottage, for his spaniel had gone to her kennel full-fed. But her five kittens still stirred feebly in the shallow scrape which she had dug for this late and last litter under the blackberry bushes.

Baldwin pushed his twenty-kilo frame into the briar fortress, his thick silvery coat armouring him against the spears and lances of the defending thorns, and dug out and ate the five babies in less than half that number of minutes. Then, clucking with pleasure, he made his rolling way to the horse chestnut's nearest neighbour, a giant grey-skinned beech tree, one of several within the wood that he used to clean and sharpen his claws upon. Its smooth bark was scored vertically to a height of a metre or more by the marks of his many visits, and he stood against the trunk and added to their number.

"That's better, Baldwin, my dear," said Baldwin, dropping back on all fours and giving himself a good shake. "That's a good start. And the night's still young so stir your stumps and let's be off again," and he trundled away through the trees.

Above him, in those trees, many of the animals of Godhanger Wood perched or sat or lay. Some were creatures of the night as he was, and heard or watched his passing as he rustled through the first-fallen leaves. Some were of the daytime and paid no heed to the badger, but slept sound and waited for the dawn.

There were birds in plenty, but there were beasts aloft too. There were bats in those trees that age or disease had hollowed, squirrels snug in their bulky dreys, and in his nest in the low crown of an ancient thickset oak there crouched a fearsome figure that peered down with eyes of coldest green at Baldwin as he snuffled noisily among the roots below, and showed its fangs in a soundless snarl. This was Gilbert the cat.

Everything about Gilbert was twisted: his corkscrew tail (caught and broken in a gin-trap), his beat-up ears, his nature. Chance survivor of a litter of farm kittens murdered by a roving cannibal tom, he viewed the world through a haze of bitterness. He had no friends amongst the woodlanders, from the smallest to the largest, from the pygmy shrew who weighed five grams to the thirty-kilo roe buck. He especially hated any invasion of his territory. Mateless, childless, friendless, Gilbert's home was all in all to him. No matter that it was only a rough hollow four metres up in the ruined oak, it was his den, and so, to his way of thinking, the tree was his and he cursed all who came near it.

Now he began to growl deep in his throat at the badger rootling below.

"Temper, temper!" cried a cheerful voice above him, and, peering up, the wild cat saw a small tubby shape perched on a branch directly over his head. It was a little owl, and at sight of this second intruder, Gilbert positively spat with anger. His green eyes glowed, and his unsheathed claws rasped on the bark at the rim of his hole in impotent fury.

"One of these nights," he hissed, "I shall kill you. Slowly."

The small squat bird, whose name was Eustace, gave a sharp bark of amusement.

"First catch your owl," he said, and then by way of comment opened wide his gape and brought up a pellet composed of mouse skin, bones and beetle fragments. The pellet narrowly missed Gilbert's head and fell to earth in front of Baldwin, who swallowed it absently before lumbering away in search of more appetizing food.

"That's more like it!" said Eustace comfortably. "I bet you wish you could do that, old moggy. It must be very unpleasant having to digest all the rubbish you eat. Probably what makes you so bad-tempered."

"I hate you," said Gilbert softly.

"That's your trouble, old moggy," said Eustace. "You hate everybody. You should try listening to someone I know."

"Who might that be?"

"He is known as the Skymaster. He is the greatest of birds."

"A bird! I should listen to a bird!"

"He is not like other birds," said Eustace.

All the time that they had been talking, Gilbert, infinitely slowly, was altering his position, inching forward from the mouth of his hole, setting his hind feet and gradually twisting his body, ready for a sudden upward pounce that would carry him the short distance to the little owl's perch, but a split second before he sprang, Eustace jumped nimbly off his branch. Striking and missing, Gilbert lost his footing and tumbled and slid all anyhow down the trunk of the oak, spitting and snarling with rage.

"Love your enemies!" shouted Eustace. "Do good to those that hate you, old moggy!" and he swooped away, quick and low, with a final burst of laughter.

CHARLOTTE'S WEB

E. B. WHITE

It is sometimes said that to give animals thoughts and feelings is absurd. Is it? Are they not sentient creatures? Do they not, like us, respond to affection, protect their young, struggle to survive? Here Wilbur the pig is feeling sad and lonely (I've seen pigs like that, and I know a happy pig when I see one!). He is longing for a friend – and friends come in all shapes and sizes, as he's about to find out.

THE NEXT DAY WAS RAINY AND DARK. Rain fell on the roof of the barn and dripped steadily from the eaves. Rain fell in the barnyard and ran in crooked courses down into the lane where thistles and pigweed grew. Rain spattered against Mrs Zuckerman's kitchen windows and came gushing out of the downspouts. Rain fell on the backs of the sheep as they grazed in the meadow. When the sheep tired of standing in the rain, they walked slowly up the lane and into the fold.

Rain upset Wilbur's plans. Wilbur had planned to go out, this day, and dig a new hole in his yard. He had other plans, too. His plans for the day went something like this:

Breakfast at six-thirty. Skim milk, crusts, middlings, bits

of doughnuts, wheat cakes with drops of maple syrup sticking to them, potato skins, left-over custard pudding with raisins, and bits of Shredded Wheat.

Breakfast would be finished at seven.

From seven to eight, Wilbur planned to have a talk with Templeton, the rat that lived under his trough. Talking with Templeton was not the most interesting occupation in the world but it was better than nothing.

From eight to nine, Wilbur planned to take a nap outdoors in the sun.

From nine to eleven, he planned to dig a hole, or trench, and possibly find something good to eat buried in the dirt.

From eleven to twelve, he planned to stand still and watch flies on the boards, watch bees in the clover, and watch swallows in the air.

Twelve o'clock – lunchtime. Middlings, warm water, apple parings, meat gravy, carrot scrapings, meat scraps, stale hominy, and the wrapper off a package of cheese. Lunch would be over at one.

From one to two, Wilbur planned to sleep.

From two to three, he planned to scratch itchy places by rubbing against the fence.

From three to four, he planned to stand perfectly still and think of what it was like to be alive, and to wait for Fern.

At four would come supper. Skim milk, provender, left-over sandwich from Lurvy's lunchbox, prune skins, a morsel of this, a bit of that, fried potatoes, marmalade drippings, a little more of this, a little more of that, a piece of baked apple, a scrap of upside-down cake.

Wilbur had gone to sleep thinking about these plans. He awoke at six and saw the rain, and it seemed as though he couldn't bear it.

"I get everything all beautifully planned out and it has to go and rain," he said.

For a while he stood gloomily indoors. Then he walked to the door and looked out. Drops of rain struck his face. His yard was cold and wet. His trough had an inch of rain water in it. Templeton was nowhere to be seen.

"Are you out there, Templeton?" called Wilbur. There was no answer. Suddenly Wilbur felt lonely and friendless.

"One day just like another," he groaned. "I'm very young, I have no real friends here in the barn, it's going to rain all morning and all afternoon, and Fern won't come in such bad weather. Oh honestly!" And Wilbur was crying again, for the second time in two days.

At six-thirty Wilbur heard the banging of a pail. Lurvy was standing outside in the rain, stirring up breakfast.

"C'mon, pig!" said Lurvy.

Wilbur did not budge. Lurvy dumped the slops, scraped the pail, and walked away. He noticed that something was wrong with the pig.

Wilbur didn't want food, he wanted love. He wanted a friend – someone who would play with him. He mentioned this to the goose, who was sitting quietly in a corner of the sheepfold.

"Will you come over and play with me?" he asked.

"Sorry, sonny, sorry," said the goose. "I'm sitting-sitting on my eggs. Eight of them. Got to keep them toasty-oasty-oasty warm. I have to stay right here, I'm no flibberty-ibberty-gibbet. I do not play when there are eggs to hatch. I'm expecting goslings."

"Well, I didn't think you were expecting woodpeckers," said Wilbur bitterly.

Wilbur next tried one of the lambs.

"Will you please play with me?" he asked.

"Certainly not," said the lamb. "In the first place, I cannot get into your pen, as I am not old enough to jump over the fence. In the second place, I am not interested in pigs. Pigs mean less than nothing to me."

"What do you mean, *less* than nothing?" replied Wilbur. "I don't think there is any such thing as *less* than nothing. Nothing is absolutely the limit of nothingness. It's the lowest you can go. It's the end of the line. How can something be less than nothing? If there were something that was less than nothing, then nothing would not be nothing, it would be something – even though it's just a very little bit of something. But if nothing is *nothing*, then nothing has nothing that is less than *it* is."

"Oh, be quiet!" said the lamb. "Go play by yourself! I don't play with pigs."

Sadly, Wilbur lay down and listened to the rain. Soon he saw the rat climbing down a slanting board that he used as a stairway.

"Will you play with me, Templeton?" asked Wilbur.

"Play?" said Templeton, twirling his whiskers. "Play? I hardly know the meaning of the word."

"Well," said Wilbur, "it means to have fun, to frolic, to run and skip and make merry."

"I never do those things if I can avoid them," replied the rat, sourly. "I prefer to spend my time eating, gnawing, spying, and hiding. I am a glutton but not a merrymaker. Right now I am on my way to your trough to eat your breakfast, since you haven't got sense enough to eat it yourself." And Templeton, the rat, crept stealthily along the wall and disappeared into a private tunnel that he had dug between the door and the trough in Wilbur's yard. Templeton was a crafty rat, and he had things pretty much his own way. The tunnel was an example of his skill and cunning. The tunnel enabled him to get from the barn to his hiding-place under the pig trough without coming out into the open. He had tunnels and runways all over Mr Zuckerman's farm and could get from one place to another without being seen. Usually he slept during the daytime and was abroad only after dark.

Wilbur watched him disappear into his tunnel. In a moment he saw the rat's sharp nose poke out from underneath the wooden trough. Cautiously Templeton pulled himself up over the edge of the trough. This was almost more than Wilbur could stand: on this dreary, rainy day to see his breakfast being eaten by somebody else. He knew Templeton was getting soaked, out there in the pouring rain, but even that didn't comfort him. Friendless, dejected, and hungry, he threw himself down in the manure and sobbed.

Late that afternoon, Lurvy went to Mr Zuckerman. "I think there's something wrong with that pig of yours. He hasn't touched his food."

"Give him two spoonfuls of sulphur and a little molasses," said Mr Zuckerman.

Wilbur couldn't believe what was happening to him when Lurvy caught him and forced the medicine down his throat. This was certainly the worst day of his life. He didn't know whether he could endure the awful loneliness any more.

Darkness settled over everything. Soon there were only shadows and the noises of the sheep chewing their cuds, and occasionally the rattle of a cow-chain up overhead. You can imagine Wilbur's surprise when, out of the darkness, came a small voice he had never heard before. It sounded rather thin, but pleasant. "Do you want a friend, Wilbur?" it said. "I'll be a friend to you. I've watched you all day and I like you."

"But I can't see you," said Wilbur, jumping to his feet. "Where are you? And *who* are you?"

"I'm right up here," said the voice. "Go to sleep. You'll see me in the morning."

* * *

The night seemed long. Wilbur's stomach was empty and his mind was full. And when your stomach is empty and your mind is full, it's always hard to sleep.

A dozen times during the night Wilbur woke and stared into the blackness, listening to the sounds and trying to figure out what time it was. A barn is never perfectly quiet. Even at midnight there is usually something stirring.

The first time he woke, he heard Templeton gnawing a hole in the grain bin. Templeton's teeth scraped loudly against the wood and made quite a racket. "That crazy rat!" thought Wilbur. "Why does he have to stay up all night, grinding his clashers and destroying people's property? Why can't he go to sleep, like any decent animal?"

The second time Wilbur woke, he heard the goose turning on her nest and chuckling to herself.

"What time is it?" whispered Wilbur to the goose.

"Probably-obably-obably about half past eleven," said the goose. "Why aren't you asleep, Wilbur?"

"Too many things on my mind," said Wilbur.

"Well," said the goose, "that's not *my* trouble. I have nothing at all on my mind, but I've too many things under my behind. Have you ever tried to sleep while sitting on eight eggs?"

"No," replied Wilbur. "I suppose it *is* uncomfortable. How long does it take a goose egg to hatch?"

"Approximately-oximately thirty days, all told," answered the goose. "But I cheat a little. On warm afternoons, I just pull a little straw over the eggs and go out for a walk."

Wilbur yawned and went back to sleep. In his dreams he heard again the voice saying, "I'll be a friend to you. Go to sleep – you'll see me in the morning."

About half an hour before dawn, Wilbur woke and listened. The barn was still dark. The sheep lay motionless.

Even the goose was quiet. Overhead, on the main floor, nothing stirred: the cows were resting, the horses dozed. Templeton had quit work and gone off somewhere on an errand. The only sound was a slight scraping noise from the rooftop, where the weathervane swung back and forth. Wilbur loved the barn when it was like this – calm and quiet, waiting for light.

"Day is almost here," he thought.

Through a small window, a faint gleam appeared. One by one the stars went out. Wilbur could see the goose a few feet away. She sat with head tucked under a wing. Then he could see the sheep and the lambs. The sky lightened.

"Oh, beautiful day, it is here at last! Today I shall find my friend."

Wilbur looked everywhere. He searched his pen thoroughly. He examined the window ledge, stared up at the ceiling. But he saw nothing new. Finally he decided he would have to speak up. He hated to break the lovely stillness of dawn by using his voice; but he couldn't think of any other way to locate the mysterious new friend who was nowhere to be seen. So Wilbur cleared his throat.

"Attention, please!" he said in a loud, firm voice. "Will the party who addressed me at bedtime last night kindly make himself or herself known by giving an appropriate sign or signal!"

Wilbur paused and listened. All the other animals lifted their heads and stared at him. Wilbur blushed. But he was determined to get in touch with his unknown friend.

"Attention, please!" he said. "I will repeat the message. Will the party who addressed me at bedtime last night kindly speak up. Please tell me where you are, if you are my friend!"

The sheep looked at each other in disgust.

"Stop your nonsense, Wilbur!" said the oldest sheep. "If

you have a new friend here, you are probably disturbing his rest; and the quickest way to spoil a friendship is to wake somebody up in the morning before he is ready. How can you be sure your friend is an early riser?"

"I beg everyone's pardon," whispered Wilbur. "I didn't mean to be objectionable."

He lay down meekly in the manure, facing the door. He did not know it, but his friend was very near. And the old sheep was right – the friend was still asleep.

Soon Lurvy appeared with slops for breakfast. Wilbur rushed out, ate everything in a hurry, and licked the trough. The sheep moved off down the lane, the gander waddled along behind them, pulling grass. And then, just as Wilbur was settling down for his morning nap, he heard again the thin voice that had addressed him the night before.

"Salutations!" said the voice.

Wilbur jumped to his feet. "Salu-*what*?" he cried.

"Salutations!" repeated the voice.

"What are *they*, and where are *you*?" screamed Wilbur. "Please, *please*, tell me where you are. And what are salutations?"

"Salutations are greetings," said the voice, "When I say 'salutations', it's just my fancy way of saying hello or good morning. Actually, it's a silly expression, and I am surprised that I used it at all. As for my whereabouts, that's easy. Look up here in the corner of the doorway! Here I am. Look, I'm waving!"

At last Wilbur saw the creature that had spoken to him in such a kindly way. Stretched across the upper part of the doorway was a big spider's web and hanging from the top of the web, head down, was a large grey spider. She was about the size of a gumdrop. She had eight legs, and she was waving one of them at Wilbur in friendly greeting. "See me now?" she asked.

"Oh, yes indeed," said Wilbur. "Yes indeed! How are you? Good morning! Salutations! Very pleased to meet you. What is your name, please? May I have your name?"

"My name," said the spider, "is Charlotte."

"Charlotte what?" asked Wilbur, eagerly.

"Charlotte A. Cavatica. But just call me Charlotte."

"I think you're beautiful," said Wilbur.

"Well, I *am* pretty," replied Charlotte. "There's no denying that. Almost all spiders are rather nice-looking. I'm not as flashy as some, but I'll do. I wish I could see you, Wilbur, as clearly as you can see me."

"Why can't you?" asked the pig. "I'm right here."

"Yes, but I'm near-sighted," replied Charlotte. "I've always been dreadfully near-sighted. It's good in some ways, not so good in others. Watch me wrap up this fly."

A fly that had been crawling along Wilbur's trough had flown up and blundered into the lower part of Charlotte's web and was tangled in the sticky threads. The fly was beating its wings furiously trying to break loose and free itself.

"First," said Charlotte, "I dive at him." She plunged head-first towards the fly. As she dropped, a tiny silken thread unwound from her rear end.

"Next, I wrap him up." She grabbed the fly, threw a few jets of silk round it, and rolled it over and over, wrapping it so that it couldn't move. Wilbur watched in horror. He could hardly believe what he was seeing, and although he detested flies he was sorry for this one.

"There!" said Charlotte. "Now I knock him out, so he'll be more comfortable." She bit the fly. "He can't feel a thing now," she remarked. "He'll make a perfect breakfast for me."

"You mean you *eat* flies?" gasped Wilbur.

"Certainly. Flies, bugs, grasshoppers, choice beetles,

moths, butterflies, tasty cockroaches, gnats, midgets, daddy-long-legs, centipedes, mosquitoes, crickets – anything that is careless enough to get caught in my web. I have to live, don't I?"

"Why, yes, of course," said Wilbur. "Do they taste good?"

"Delicious. Of course, I don't really eat them. I drink them – drink their blood. I love blood," said Charlotte, and her pleasant, thin voice grew even thinner and more pleasant.

"Don't say that!" groaned Wilbur. "Please don't say things like that!"

"Why not? It's true, and I have to say what is true. I am not entirely happy about my diet of flies and bugs, but it's the way I'm made. A spider has to pick up a living somehow or other, and I happen to be a trapper. I just naturally build a web and trap flies and other insects. My mother was a trapper before me. Her mother was a trapper before her. All our family have been trappers. Way back for thousands and thousands of years we spiders have been laying for flies and bugs."

"It's a miserable inheritance," said Wilbur, gloomily. He was sad because his new friend was so bloodthirsty.

"Yes, it is," agreed Charlotte. "But I can't help it. I don't know how the first spider in the early days of the world happened to think up this fancy idea of spinning a web, but she did, and it was clever of her, too. And since then, all of us spiders have had to work the same trick. It's not a bad pitch, on the whole."

"It's cruel," replied Wilbur, who did not intend to be argued out of his position.

"Well, *you* can't talk," said Charlotte. "You have your meals brought to you in a pail. Nobody feeds me. I have to get my own living. I live by my wits. I have to be sharp and clever, lest I go hungry. I have to think things out, catch what I can, take what comes. And it just so happens, my friend, that what comes is flies and insects and bugs. And *further*more," said Charlotte, shaking one of her legs, "do you realize that if I didn't catch bugs and eat them, bugs would increase and multiply and get so numerous that they'd destroy the earth, wipe out everything?"

"Really?" said Wilbur. "I wouldn't want *that* to happen. Perhaps your web is a good thing after all."

The goose had been listening to this conversation and chuckling to herself. "There are a lot of things Wilbur doesn't know about life," she thought. "He's really a very innocent little pig. He doesn't even know what's going to happen to him around Christmastime; he has no idea that Mr Zuckerman and Lurvy are plotting to kill him." And the goose raised herself a bit and poked her eggs a little farther under her so that they would receive the full heat from her warm body and soft feathers.

Charlotte stood quietly over the fly, preparing to eat it. Wilbur lay down and closed his eyes. He was tired from his wakeful night and from the excitement of meeting someone for the first time. A breeze brought him the smell of clover – the sweet-smelling world beyond his fence. "Well," he thought, "I've got a new friend, all right. But what a gamble friendship is! Charlotte is fierce, brutal, scheming, bloodthirsty – everything I don't like. How can I learn to like her, even though she is pretty and, of course, clever?"

Wilbur was merely suffering the doubts and fears that often go with finding a new friend. In good time he was to discover that he was mistaken about Charlotte. Underneath her rather bold and cruel exterior, she had a kind heart, and she was to prove loyal and true to the very end.

TARKA THE OTTER

HENRY WILLIAMSON

Henry Williamson lived very near where I live in Devon. He walked the same rivers, saw the herons, the barn owls, the kingfishers that I see. So close is he to the creatures he writes about that we feel we are swimming alongside Tarka in the Torridge. We feel his terror as Deadlock comes hunting.

HE WAS AWAKENED by the tremendous baying of hounds. He saw feet splashing in the shallow water, a row of noses, and many flacking tongues. The entrance was too small for any head to enter. He crouched a yard away, against the cold rock. The noise hurt the fine drums of his ears.

Hob-nailed boots scraped on the brown shillets of the waterbed, and iron-tipped hunting poles tapped the rocks.

Go'r'n leave it! Leave it! Go'r'n leave it! Deadlock! Harper! Go'r'n leave it!

Tarka heard the horn and the low opening became lighter.

Go'r'n leave it! Captain! Deadlock! Go'r'n leave it!

The horn twanged fainter as the pack was taken away.

Then a pole was thrust into the holt and prodded about blindly. It slid out again. Tarka saw boots and hands and the face of a terrier. A voice whispered, *Leu in there, Sammy, leu in there!* The small ragged brown animal crept out of the hands. Sammy smelled Tarka, saw him and began to sidle towards him. *Waugh-waugh-waugh-wa-waugh.* As the otter did not move, the terrier crept nearer to him, yapping with head stretched forward.

After a minute, Tarka could bear the irritating noises no more. Tissing, with open mouth, he moved past the terrier, whose snarly yapping changed to a high-pitched yelping. The men on the opposite bank stood silent and still. They saw Tarka's head in sunlight, which came through the trees behind them and turned the brown shillets a warm yellow. The water ran clear and cold. Tarka saw three men in blue coats; they did not move and he slipped into the water. It did not cover his back, and he returned to the bankside roots. He moved in the shadows and under the ferns at his ordinary travelling pace. One of three watching men declared that an otter had no sense of fear.

No hound spoke, but the reason of the silence was not considered by Tarka, who could not reason such things. He had been awakened with a shock, he had been tormented by a noise, he had left a dangerous place, and he was escaping from human enemies. As he walked upstream, with raised head, his senses of smell, sight, and hearing were alert for his greatest enemies, the hounds.

The stream being narrow and shallow, the otter was given four minutes' law. Four minutes after Tarka had left he heard behind him the short and long notes of the horn, and the huntsman crying amidst the tongues of hounds *Ol-ol-ol-ol-ol-ol-over! Get on to 'm! Ol-ol-ol-ol-over!* as the pack returned in full cry to the water. Hounds splashed into the water around the rock, wedging themselves at its opening and breaking into couples and half-couples, leaping through the water after the wet and shivering terrier, throwing their tongues and dipping their noses to the wash of scent coming down.

Deadlock plunged at the lead, with Coraline, Sailoress, Captain, and Playboy. They passed the terrier, and Deadlock was so eager that he knocked him down. Sammy picked up his shivery body and followed.

Tarka sank all but his nostrils in a pool and waited. He lay in the sunlit water like a brown log slanting to the stones on which his rudder rested. The huntsman saw him. Tarka lifted his whiskered head out of the water, and stared at the huntsman. Hounds were speaking just below. From the pool the stream flowed for six feet down the smooth slide up which he had crept. When Deadlock jumped into the pool and lapped the scent lying on the water, Tarka put down his head with hardly a ripple, and like a skin of brown oil moved under the hound's belly. Soundlessly he emerged, and the sun glistened on his water-sleeked coat as he walked down on the algae-smeared rock. He seemed to walk under their muzzles slowly, and to be treading on their feet.

Let hounds hunt him! Don't help hounds or they'll chop him!

The pack was confused. Every hound owned the scent, which was like a tangled line, the end of which was sought for unravelling. But soon Deadlock pushed through the pack and told the way the otter had gone.

As Tarka was running over shillets with water scarcely deep enough to cover his rudder, Deadlock saw him and with stiff stern ran straight at him. Tarka quitted the water. The dead twigs and leaves at the hedge-bottom crackled and rustled as he pushed through to the meadow. While he was running over the grass, he could hear the voice of Deadlock raging as the bigger black-and-white hound

struggled though the hazel twigs and brambles and honeysuckle bines. He crossed fifty yards of meadow, climbed the bank, and ran down again on to a tarred road. The surface burned his pads, but he ran on, and even when an immense crimson creature bore down upon him he did not go back into the meadow across which hounds were streaming. With a series of shudders the crimson creature slowed to a standstill, while human figures rose out of it, and pointed. He ran under the motor-coach, and came out into brown sunshine, hearing above the shouts of men the clamour of hounds trying to scramble up the high bank and pulling each other down in their eagerness.

He ran in the shade of the ditch, among bits of newspaper, banana and orange skins, cigarette ends and crushed chocolate boxes. A long yellow creature grew bigger and bigger before him, and women rose out of it and peered down at him as he passed it. With smarting eyes he ran two hundred yards of the road, which for him was a place of choking stinks and hurtful noises. Pausing in the ditch, he harkened to the clamour changing its tone as hounds leaped down into the road. He ran on for another two hundred yards, then climbed the bank, pushed through dusty leaves and grasses and briars that would hold him, and down the sloping meadow to the stream. He splashed into the water and swam until rocks and boulders rose before him. He climbed and walked over them. His rudder drawn on mosses and lichen left a strong scent behind him. Deadlock, racing over the green-shadowed grassland, threw his tongue before the pack.

In the water, through shallow and pool, his pace was steady, but not hurried; he moved faster than the stream; he insinuated himself from slide to pool, from pool to boulder, leaving his scent in the wet marks of his pads and rudder.

People were running through the meadow, and in the near distance arose the notes of the horn and hoarse cries. Hounds' tongues broke out united and firm, and Tarka knew that they had reached the stream. The sun-laden water of the pools was spun into eddies by the thrusts of his webbed hindlegs. He passed through shadow and dapple, through runnel and plash. The water sparkled amber in the sunbeams, and his brown sleek pelt glistened whenever his back made ripples. His movements in water were unhurried, like an eel's. The hounds came nearer.

The stream after a bend flowed near the roadway, where more motor-cars were drawn up. Some men and women, holding notched poles, were watching from the cars – sportsmen on wheels.

Beggars' Roost Bridge was below. With hounds so near Tarka was heedless of the men that leaned over the stone parapet, watching for him. They shouted, waved hats, and cheered the hounds. There were ducks above the bridge, quacking loudly as they left the stream and waddled to the yard, and when Tarka came to where they had been, he left the water and ran after them. They beat their wings as they tried to fly from him, but he reached the file and scattered them, running through them and disappearing. Nearer and nearer came Deadlock, with Captain and Waterwitch leading the pack. Huntsman, whippers-in, and field were left behind, struggling through hedges and over banks.

Hounds were bewildered when they reached the yard. They ran with noses to ground in puzzled excitement. Captain's shrill voice told that Tarka had gone under a gate. Waterwitch followed the wet seals in the dust, but turned off along a track of larger webs. The line was tangled again. Deadlock threw his belving tongue. Other hounds followed, but the scent led only to a duck that beat its wings and quacked in terror before them. A man with a rake drove them off, shouting and threatening to strike them. Dewdrop spoke across the yard and the hounds galloped to her, but the line led to a gate which they tried to leap, hurling themselves up and falling from the top bar. A duck had gone under the gate, but not Tarka.

All scent was gone. Hounds rolled in the dust or trotted up to men and women, sniffing their pockets for food. Rufus found a rabbit skin and ate it; Render fought with Sandboy – but not seriously, as they feared each other; Deadlock went off alone. And hounds were waiting for a lead when the sweating huntsman, "white" pot-hat pushed back from his red brow, ran up with the two whippers-in and called them into a pack again. The thick scent of Muscovy ducks had checked the hunt.

Tarka had run through a drain back to the stream, and now he rested in the water that carried him every moment nearer to the murderous glooms of the glen below. He saw the coloured blur of a kingfisher perching on a twig as it eyed the water for beetle or loach. The kingfisher saw him moving under the surface, as his shadow broke the net of ripple shadows that drifted in meshes of pale gold on the stony bed beneath him.

While he was walking past the roots of a willow under the bank, he heard the yapping of the terrier. Sammy had crept through the drain, and was looking out at the end, covered with black filth, and eagerly telling his big friends to follow him downstream. As he yapped, Deadlock threw his tongue. The stallion hound was below the drain, and had re-found the line where Tarka had last touched the shillets. Tarka saw him ten yards away, and slipping back into the water, swam with all webs down the current, pushing from his nose a ream whose shadow beneath was an arrow of gold pointing down to the sea.

Again he quitted the water and ran on land to wear away

his scent. He had gone twenty yards when Deadlock scrambled up the bank with Render and Sandboy, breathing the scent which was as high as their muzzles. Tarka reached the waterside trees again a length ahead of Deadlock, and fell into the water like a sodden log. Deadlock leapt after him and snapped at his head; but the water was friendly to the otter, who rolled in smooth and graceful movement away from the jaws, a straight bite of which would have crushed his skull.

Here sunlight was shut out by the oaks, and the roar of the first fall was beating back from the leaves. The current ran faster, narrowing into a race with twirls and hollows marking the sunken rocks. The roar grew louder in a drifting spray. Tarka and Deadlock were carried to where a broad sunbeam came down through a break in the foliage and lit the mist above the fall. Tarka went over in the heavy white folds of the torrent and Deadlock was hurled over after him. They were lost in the churn and pressure of the pool until a small brown head appeared and gazed for its enemy in the broken honeycomb of foam. A black and white body uprolled beside it, and the head of the hound was thrust up as he tried to tread away from the current that would draw him under. Tarka was master of whirlpools; they were his playthings. He rocked in the surge with delight; then high above he heard the note of the horn. He yielded himself to the water and let it take him away down the gorge into a pool where rocks were piled above. He searched under the dripping ferny clitter for a hiding place.

Under water he saw two legs, joined to two wavering and inverted images of legs, and above them the blurred shapes of a man's head and shoulders. He turned away from the fisherman into the current again, and as he breathed he heard the horn again. On the road above the glen the pack was trotting between huntsman and whippers-in, and before them men were running with poles at the trail, hurrying down the hill to the bridge, to make a stickle to stop Tarka reaching the sea.

Tarka left Deadlock far behind. The hound was feeble and bruised and breathing harshly, his head battered and his sight dazed, but still following. Tarka passed another fisherman, and by chance the tiny feathered hook lodged in his ear. The reel spun against the check, *re-re-re* continuously, until all the silken line had run through the snake-rings of the rod, which bent into a circle, and whipped back straight again as the gut trace snapped.

Tarka saw the bridge, the figure of a man below it, and a row of faces above. He heard shouts. The man standing on a rock took off his hat, scooped the air, and holla'd to the huntsman, who was running and slipping with the pack on the loose stones of the steep red road. Tarka walked out of the last pool above the bridge, ran over a mossy rock merged with the water again, and pushed through the legs of the man.

Tally Ho!

Tarka had gone under the bridge when Harper splashed into the water. The pack poured through the gap between the end of the parapet and the hillside earth, and their tongues rang under the bridge and down the walls of the houses built on the rock above the river.

Among rotting motor tyres, broken bottles, tins, pails, shoes, and other castaway rubbish lying in the bright water, hounds made their plunging leaps. Once Tarka turned back; often he was splashed and trodden on. The stream was seldom deep enough to cover him, and always shallow enough for the hounds to move at double his speed. Sometimes he was under the pack, and then, while hounds were massing for the worry, his small head would look out beside a rock ten yards below them.

Between boulders and rocks crusted with shellfish and shaggy with seaweed, past worm-channered posts that marked the fairway for fishing boats at high water, the pack hunted the otter. Off each post a gull launched itself, cackling angrily as it looked down at the animals. Tarka reached the sea. He walked slowly into the surge of a wavelet, and sank away from the chop of old Harper's jaws, just as Deadlock ran through the pack. Hounds swam beyond the line of waves, while people stood at the sea-lap and watched the huntsman wading to his waist. It was said that the otter was dead-beat, and probably floating stiffly in the shallow water. After a few minutes the huntsman shook his head, and withdrew the horn from his waistcoat. He filled his lungs and stopped his breath and was tightening his lips for the four long notes of the call-off, when a brown head with hard dark eyes, was thrust out of the water a yard from Deadlock. Tarka stared into the hound's face and cried *Ic-yang!*

The head sank. Swimming under Deadlock, Tarka bit on to the loose skin of the flews and pulled the hound's head under water. Deadlock tried to twist round and crush the otter's skull in his jaws, but he struggled vainly. Bubbles blew out of his mouth. Soon he was choking. The hounds did not know what was happening. Deadlock's hindlegs kicked the air weakly. The huntsman waded out and pulled him inshore, but Tarka loosened his bite only when he needed new air in his lungs; and then he swam under and gripped Deadlock again. Only when hounds were upon him did Tarka let go. He vanished in a wave.

Long after the water had been emptied out of Deadlock's lungs, and the pack had trotted off for the long uphill climb to the railway station, the gulls were flying over something in the sea beyond the mouth of the little estuary.

Sometimes one dropped its yellow webs to alight on the water; always it flew up again into the restless, wailing throng, startled by the snaps of white teeth. A cargo steamer was passing up the Severn Sea, leaving a long smudge of smoke on the horizon, where a low line of clouds billowed over the coast of Wales. The regular thumps of its screws in the windless blue calm were borne to where Tarka lay, drowsy and content, but watching the pale yellow eyes of the nearest bird. At last the gulls grew tired of seeing only his eyes, and flew back to their posts; and turning on his back, Tarka yawned and stretched himself, and floated at his ease.

THE OLD MAN AND THE SEA

ERNEST HEMINGWAY

This is the most extraordinary evocation of the respect of the hunter for the hunted, of a man's closeness to the world about him. To me there is no cruelty here, only empathy.

WHEN THE SUN HAD RISEN FURTHER the old man realized that the fish was not tiring. There was only one favourable sign. The slant of the line showed he was swimming at a lesser depth. That did not necessarily mean that he would jump. But he might.

"God let him jump," the old man said. "I have enough line to handle him."

Maybe if I can increase the tension just a little it will hurt him and he will jump, he thought. Now that it is daylight let him jump so that he'll fill the sacs along his backbone with air and then he cannot go deep to die.

He tried to increase the tension, but the line had been taut up to the very edge of the breaking point since he had hooked the fish and he felt the harshness as he leaned back to pull and knew he could put no more strain on it. I must not jerk it ever, he thought. Each jerk widens the cut the hook makes and then when he does jump he might throw it. Anyway I feel better with the sun and for once I do not have to look into it.

There was yellow weed on the line but the old man knew that only made an added drag and he was pleased. It was the yellow Gulf weed that had made so much phosphorescence in the night.

"Fish," he said, "I love you and respect you very much. But I will kill you dead before this day ends."

Let us hope so, he thought.

A small bird came toward the skiff from the north. He was a warbler and flying very low over the water. The old man could see that he was very tired.

The bird made the stern of the boat and rested there. Then he flew around the old man's head and rested on the line where he was more comfortable.

"How old are you?" the old man asked the bird. "Is this your first trip?"

The bird looked at him when he spoke. He was too tired even to examine the line and he teetered on it as his delicate feet gripped it fast.

"It's steady," the old man told him. "It's too steady. You shouldn't be that tired after a windless night. What are birds coming to?"

The hawks, he thought, that come out to sea to meet them. But he said nothing of this to the bird who could not understand him anyway and who would learn about the hawks soon enough.

"Take a good rest, small bird," he said. "Then go in and take your chance like any man or bird or fish."

It encouraged him to talk because his back had stiffened in the night and it hurt truly now.

"Stay at my house if you like, bird," he said. "I am sorry I cannot hoist the sail and take you in with the small breeze that is rising. But I am with a friend."

Just then the fish gave a sudden lurch that pulled the old man down on to the bow and would have pulled him overboard if he had not braced himself and given some line.

The bird had flown up when the line jerked and the old man had not even seen him go. He felt the line carefully with his right hand and noticed his hand was bleeding.

"Something hurt him then," he said aloud and pulled back on the line to see if he could turn the fish. But when he was touching the breaking point he held steady and settled back against the strain of the line.

"You're feeling it now, fish," he said. "And so, God knows, am I."

He looked around for the bird now because he would have liked him for company. The bird was gone.

You did not stay long, the man thought. But it is rougher where you are going until you make the shore. How did I let the fish cut me with that one quick pull he made? I must be getting very stupid. Or perhaps I was looking at the small bird and thinking of him. Now I will pay attention to my work and then I must eat the tuna so that I will not have a failure of strength.

"I wish the boy were here and that I had some salt," he said aloud.

Shifting the weight of the line to his left shoulder and kneeling carefully he washed his hand in the ocean and held it there, submerged, for more than a minute watching the blood trail away and the steady movement of the water against his hand as the boat moved.

"He has slowed much," he said.

The old man would have liked to keep his hand in the salt water longer but he was afraid of another sudden lurch by the fish and he stood up and braced himself and held his hand up against the sun. It was only a line burn that had cut his flesh. But it was in the working part of his hand. He knew he would need his hands before this was over and he did not like to be cut before it started.

"Now," he said, when his hand had dried, "I must eat the small tuna. I can reach him with the gaff and eat him here in comfort."

He knelt down and found the tuna under the stern with the gaff and drew it toward him keeping it clear of the coiled lines. Holding the line with his left shoulder again, and bracing on his left hand and arm, he took the tuna off the gaff hook and put the gaff back in place. He put one knee on the fish and cut strips of dark red meat longitudinally from the back of the head to the tail. They were wedge-shaped strips and he cut them from next to the backbone down to the edge of the belly. When he had cut six strips he spread them out on the wood of the bow, wiped his knife on his trousers, and lifted the carcass of the bonito by the tail and dropped it overboard.

"I don't think I can eat an entire one," he said and drew his knife across one of the strips. He could feel the steady hard pull of the line and his left hand was cramped. It drew up tight on the heavy cord and he looked at it in disgust.

"What kind of a hand is that," he said. "Cramp then if you want. Make yourself into a claw. It will do you no good."

Come on, he thought and looked down into the dark water at the slant of the line. Eat it now and it will strengthen the hand. It is not the hand's fault and you have been many hours with the fish. But you can stay with him for ever. Eat the bonito now.

He picked up a piece and put it in his mouth and chewed it slowly. It was not unpleasant.

Chew it well, he thought, and get all the juices. It would not be bad to eat with a little lime or with lemon or with salt.

"How do you feel, hand?" he asked the cramped hand that was almost as stiff as rigor mortis. "I'll eat some more for you."

He ate the other part of the piece that he had cut in two. He chewed it carefully and then spat out the skin.

"How does it go, hand? Or is it too early to know?"

He took another full piece and chewed it.

"It is a strong full-blooded fish," he thought. "I was lucky to get him instead of dolphin. Dolphin is too sweet. This is hardly sweet at all and all the strength is still in it."

There is no sense in being anything but practical though, he thought. I wish I had some salt. And I do not know whether the sun will rot or dry what is left, so I had better eat it all although I am not hungry. The fish is calm and steady. I will eat it all and then I will be ready.

"Be patient, hand," he said. "I do this for you."

I wish I could feed the fish, he thought. He is my brother. But I must kill him and keep strong to do it. Slowly and conscientiously he ate all of the wedge-shaped strips of fish.

He straightened up, wiping his hand on his trousers.

"Now," he said. "You can let the cord go, hand, and I will handle him with the right arm alone until you stop that nonsense." He put his left foot on the heavy line that the left hand had held and lay back against the pull against his back.

"God help me to have the cramp go," he said. "Because I do not know what the fish is going to do."

But he seems calm, he thought, and following his plan. But what is his plan, he thought. And what is mine? Mine I must improvise to his because of his great size. If he will jump I can kill him. But he stays down for ever. Then I will stay down with him for ever.

He rubbed the cramped hand against his trousers and

tried to gentle the fingers. But it would not open. Maybe it will open with the sun, he thought. Maybe it will open when the strong raw tuna is digested. If I have to have it, I will open it, cost whatever it costs. But I do not want to open it now by force. Let it open by itself and come back of its own accord. After all I abused it much in the night when it was necessary to free and unite the various lines.

He looked across the sea and knew how alone he was now. But he could see the prisms in the deep dark water and the line stretching ahead and the strange undulation of the calm. The clouds were building up now for the trade wind and he looked ahead and saw a flight of wild ducks etching themselves against the sky over the water, then blurring, then etching again and he knew no man was ever alone on the sea.

He thought of how some men feared being out of sight of land in a small boat and knew they were right in the months of sudden bad weather. But now they were in hurricane months and, when there are no hurricanes, the weather of hurricane months is the best of all the year.

If there is a hurricane you always see the signs of it in the sky for days ahead, if you are at sea. They do not see it ashore because they do not know what to look for, he thought. The land must make a difference too, in the shape of the clouds. But we have no hurricane coming now.

He looked at the sky and saw the white cumulus built like friendly piles of ice cream and high above were the thin feathers of the cirrus against the high September sky.

"Light *brisa,*" he said. "Better weather for me than for you, fish."

His left hand was still cramped, but he was unknotting it slowly.

I hate a cramp, he thought. It is a treachery of one's own body. It is humiliating before others to have a diarrhoea from ptomaine poisoning or to vomit from it. But a cramp, he thought of it as a *calambre*, humiliates oneself especially when one is alone.

If the boy were here he could rub it for me and loosen it down from the forearm, he thought. But it will loosen up.

Then, with his right hand he felt the difference in the pull of the line before he saw the slant change in the water. Then, as he leaned against the line and slapped his left hand hard and fast against his thigh he saw the line slanting slowly upwards.

"He's coming up," he said. "Come on hand. Please come on."

The line rose slowly and steadily and then the surface of the ocean bulged ahead of the boat and the fish came out. He came out unendingly and water poured from his sides. He was bright in the sun and his head and back were dark purple and in the sun the stripes on his sides showed wide and a light lavender. His sword was as long as a baseball bat and tapered like a rapier and he rose his full length from the water and then re-entered it, smoothly, like a diver and the old man saw the great scythe-blade of his tail go under and the line commenced to race out.

"He is two feet longer than the skiff," the old man said. The line was going out fast but steadily and the fish was not panicked. The old man was trying with both hands to keep the line just inside of breaking strength. He knew that if he could not slow the fish with a steady pressure the fish could take out all the line and break it.

He is a great fish and I must convince him, he thought. I must never let him learn his strength nor what he could do if he made his run. If I were him I would put in everything now and go until something broke. But, thank God, they are not as intelligent as we who kill them; although they are more noble and more able.

The old man had seen many great fish. He had seen many that weighed more than a thousand pounds and he had caught two of that size in his life, but never alone. Now alone, and out of sight of land, he was fast to the biggest fish that he had ever seen and bigger than he had ever heard of, and his left hand was still as tight as the gripped claws of an eagle.

It will uncramp though, he thought. Surely it will uncramp to help my right hand. There are three things that are brothers: the fish and my two hands. It must uncramp. It is unworthy of it to be cramped. The fish had slowed again and was going at his usual pace.

I wonder why he jumped, the old man thought. He jumped almost as though to show me how big he was. I know now, anyway, he thought. I wish I could show him what sort of man I am. But then he would see the cramped hand. Let him think I am more man than I am and I will be so. I wish I was the fish, he thought, with everything he has against only my will and my intelligence.

He settled comfortably against the wood and took his suffering as it came and the fish swam steadily and the boat moved slowly through the dark water. There was a small sea rising with the wind coming up from the east and at noon the old man's left hand was uncramped.

"Bad news for you, fish," he said and shifted the line over the sacks that covered his shoulders.

He was comfortable but suffering, although he did not admit the suffering at all.

"I am not religious," he said. "But I will say ten Our Fathers and ten Hail Marys that I should catch this fish, and I promise to make a pilgrimage to the Virgin de Cobre if I catch him. That is a promise."

He commenced to say his prayers mechanically. Sometimes he would be so tired that he could not remember the prayer and then he would say them fast so that they would come automatically. Hail Marys are easier to say then Our Fathers, he thought.

"Hail Mary full of Grace the Lord is with thee. Blessed art thou among women and blessed is the fruit of thy womb, Jesus. Holy Mary, Mother of God, pray for us sinners now and at the hour of our death. Amen." Then he added, "Blessed Virgin, pray for the death of this fish. Wonderful though he is."

With his prayers said, and feeling much better, but suffering exactly as much, and perhaps a little more, he leaned against the wood of the bow and began, mechanically, to work the fingers of his left hand.

The sun was hot now although the breeze was rising gently.

"I had better re-bait that little line out over the stern," he said. "If the fish decides to stay another night I will need to eat again and the water is low in the bottle. I don't think I can get anything but a dolphin here. But if I eat him fresh enough he won't be too bad. I wish a flying fish would come on board tonight. But I have no light to attract them. A flying fish is excellent to eat raw and I would not have to cut him up. I must save all my strength now. Christ, I did not know he was so big."

"I'll kill him though," he said. "In all his greatness and his glory."

Although it is unjust, he thought. But I will show him what a man can do and what a man endures.

THE IRON WOMAN

TED HUGHES

Now a piece from Ted Hughes' powerful ecological tale: a dread warning that we despoil, destroy and pollute the world about us at our peril, for we are an integral part of it.

The Iron Woman is the harbinger of this message – and Lucy is about to meet her. Lucy has just woken from a terrible nightmare, the latch rattling at her door, a seal-like face peering down at her, begging her to wake up. Outside "she could see a gigantic shape towering there in the darkness", a shape that seems to be beckoning her outside.

LUCY EASED OPEN THE FRONT DOOR and looked out. Her heart was pounding. What was she going to see? A person on top of a vehicle? Or on top of one of those cranes they use for repairing streetlights? Or simply a colossal person with those immense fingers? Whatever it was, the three snowdrops had been real enough. But the street was empty.

Now she was outside, the world seemed not quite so dark. Already, behind the roofs to the east, the inky sky had paled a little. She closed the door behind her and stood a moment, listening. She realized she was hearing a skylark, far up. Somewhere on the other side of the village a thrush sang a first few notes. But the great shape had vanished.

Then something brushed her face lightly and fell to the ground. She picked it up. A foxglove.

At the same moment, she smelt a dreadful, half-rotten smell. She knew it straightaway: the smell of the mud of the marsh. She thought it came from the foxglove. But no, it filled the whole air, and she looked upwards.

An immense dark head with two huge eyes was looking down at her, round the end of the house. It must be standing in the driveway, she thought, in front of the garage.

Lucy walked slowly round the end of the house, gazing up. And there it was. Not standing, but sitting – its back to the house wall. And here was the smell all right. This immense creature seemed to be made entirely of black slime, with reeds and tendrils of roots clinging all over. Lucy simply stared up at the face that stared down at her. She felt a wild excitement, as if she were travelling at the most tremendous speed. Had this thing come from the sea, and waded through the marsh? She remembered the face like a seal's in her nightmare, the girl's face with eyes like a seal, and then very sharp and clear that voice crying: "Clean me." Had it said: "Clean me"? Was this what the snowdrops meant?

Lucy knew exactly what to do. She unrolled her father's hosepipe, which was already fitted to an outside tap, turned the tap full on, and pressed her finger half over the nozzle to make a stiff jet.

It was then she thought she heard another voice, a soft, rumbling voice. Like far-off thunder. She could not be sure where it came from. A strange voice. At least, it had a strange effect on Lucy. It made her feel safe and bold. And she seemed to hear:

"Waste no time."

The moment the jet hit the nearest leg she saw the bright gloss beneath. It looked like metal – polished black metal. The mud sluiced off easily. But it was a big job. And Lucy was thinking: What are people going to think when it gets light and they see this? She washed the nearest leg, the giant foot, the peculiar toes. She hosed between the toes. This first leg took about as much hosing as an entire car.

The voice came again, so low it seemed to vibrate inside her:

"Hurry!"

A faint tinge of pink outlined the chimneys to the east. Already it seemed that every single bird in the village must be singing. A van went past.

Lucy switched the jet to the face. It was an awesome face, like a great, black, wet mudpack. Then the giant hand opened palm upwards, flat on the driveway. Lucy saw what was wanted. She stepped on to the hand, which lifted her close to the face.

The jet sizzled into the deep crevices around the tightly closed eyes and over the strange curves of the cheeks. As she angled the jet to the massively folded shape of the lips, the eyes opened, brilliantly black, and beamed at her. Then Lucy saw that this huge being was a woman. It was exactly as if the rigid jet of water were carving this gleaming, black, giant woman out of a cliff of black clay. Last, she drove the slicing water into the hair – huge coils of wires in a complicated arrangement. And the great face closed its eyes and opened its mouth and laughed softly.

Lucy could see the muddy water splashing on to the white, pebble-dashed wall of the house and realized it was almost daylight. She turned, and saw a red-hot cinder of sun between two houses. A lorry thumped past. She knew then that she wasn't going to get this job finished.

At the same moment, still holding Lucy in her hand, the

giant figure heaved upright. Lucy knew that the voice had rumbled, somewhere: "More water." She dropped the hose, which writhed itself into a comfortable position and went on squirting over the driveway.

"There's the canal," she said.

The other great hand pushed her gently, till she lay in the crook of the huge arm, like a very small doll. This was no time to bother about the mud or the smell of it. She saw the light of her own bedroom go past, slightly below her, the window still open, as the giant woman turned up the street.

When they reached the canal, and stood on the bridge looking down, Lucy suddenly felt guilty. For some reason, it was almost empty of water, as she had never seen it before. A long, black, oily puddle lay between slopes of drying grey mud. And embedded in the mud were rusty bicycle wheels, supermarket trolleys, bedsteads, prams, old refrigerators, washing machines, car batteries, even two or three old cars, along with hundreds of rusty, twisted odds and ends, tangles of wire, cans and bottles and plastic bags. They both stared for a while. Lucy felt she was seeing this place for the first time. It looked like a canal only when it was full of water. Now it was nearly empty, it was obviously a rubbish dump.

"The river," came the low, rumbling voice, vibrating Lucy's whole body where she lay.

The river ran behind a strip of woodland, a mile away across the fields. That was a strange ride for Lucy. The sun had risen and hung clear, a red ball. She could see a light on in a farmhouse. A flock of sheep and lambs poured wildly into a far corner. Any second she expected to hear a shout.

But they reached the strip of trees. And there was the river. It swirled past, cold and unfriendly in the early light.

The hand set Lucy down among the weeds of the bank, and she watched amazed as the gigantic figure waded out into midstream, till the water bulged and bubbled past those thighs that were like the pillars of a bridge. There, in the middle of the river, the giant woman kneeled, bowed, and plunged under the surface. For a moment, a great mound of foaming water heaved up. Then the head and shoulders hoisted clear, glistening black, and plunged under again, like the launching of a ship. Waves slopped over the bank and soaked Lucy to the knees. For a few minutes, it was like a giant sea beast out there, rearing up and plunging back under, in a boiling of muddy water.

Then abruptly the huge woman levered herself upright and came ashore. All the mud had been washed from her body. She shone like black glass. But her great face seemed to writhe. As if in pain. She spat out water and a groan came rumbling from her.

"It's washed you," cried Lucy. "You're clean!"

But the face went on trying to spit out water, even though it had no more water to spit.

"It burns!" Lucy heard. "It burns!" And the enormous jointed fingers, bunched into fists, rubbed and squeezed at her eyes.

Lucy could now see her clearly in full daylight. She gazed at the giant tubes of the limbs, the millions of rivets, the funny concertinas at the joints. It was hard to believe what she was seeing.

"Are you a robot?" she cried.

Perhaps, she thought, somebody far off is controlling this creature, from a panel of dials. Perhaps she's a sort of human-shaped submarine. Perhaps . . .

But the rumbling voice came up out of the ground, through Lucy's legs:

"I am not a robot," it said. "I am the real thing."

And now the face was looking at her. The huge eyes, huge black pupils, seemed to enclose Lucy – like the gentle grasp of a warm hand. The whole body was like a robot, but the face was somehow different. It was like some colossal metal statue's face, made of parts that slid over each other as they moved. Now the lips opened again, and Lucy almost closed her eyes, she almost shivered, in the peculiar vibration of the voice:

"I am Iron Woman."

"Iron Woman!" whispered Lucy, staring at her again.

"And you are wondering why I have come," the voice went on.

Lucy nodded.

"Because of this!" The voice was suddenly louder, and angry. Lucy winced, as the eyes opened even wider, larger, glaring at her.

"What? Because of what?" Lucy had no idea.

"Listen," rumbled the voice.

Lucy listened. By now, the whole land, inside the circle of the horizon, was simmering and bubbling with birdsong, like a great pan.

The birds?" she asked. "I can hear –"

"No!" And the black eyes flashed. A red light pulsed in their depths. Lucy felt suddenly afraid. What did she mean?

"Listen – listen –" The rumbling voice almost cracked into a kind of yell. A great hand had come out now and folded round Lucy's shoulders, just as her father would put his arm around her, while the other hand, with that colossal finger and thumb, just as daintily as it had held the snowdrops, took hold of her hand and gripped it, softly but firmly.

Lucy's fright lasted only for a second. Then she was overwhelmed by what she heard. A weird, horrible sound.

A roar of cries. Thousands, millions of cries – wailings, groans, screams. She closed her eyes and put her free hand over her ear. But it made no difference. The dreadful sound seemed to pound her body, as if she were standing under a waterfall of it, as if it might batter her off her feet. Or as if she were standing in a railway tunnel, and the express train was rushing towards her, an express of screaming voices –

Finally, she could stand it no longer and she actually screamed herself. She opened her eyes, trying to drag her hand free and to twist free of the hand enclosing her shoulders. But the thumb and finger held her too tightly, and the enfolding hand gripped her too firmly. And all the time the immense black eyes, so round and so fixed, stared at her. And even though her own eyes were wide open that horrible mass of screams, yells, wails, groans came hurtling closer and closer, louder and louder – till she knew that in the next moment it would hit her like that express train and sweep her away.

But at that moment, the fingers and the hand let her go, and the sound stopped. As if a switch had switched it off.

Lucy stood panting with fear. She almost started to run – anywhere away from where she had been standing. But the great eyes, now half-closed, had become gentle again.

"Oh, what was it?" cried Lucy. "Oh, how awful!" She felt herself trembling and knew she might burst into tears. Her ears were still ringing.

"What you heard," said the voice, "is what I am hearing all the time."

"But what is it?" cried Lucy again.

"That," said the voice, "is the cry of the marsh. It is the cry of the insects, the leeches, the worms, the shrimps, the water skeeters, the beetles, the bream, the perch, the carp, the pike, the eels."

"They're crying." whispered Lucy.

"The cry of the ditches and the ponds," the voice went on. "Of the frogs, the toads, the newts. The cry of the rivers and the lakes. Of all the creatures under the water, on top of the water, and all that go between. The waterbirds, the water voles, the water shrews, the otters. Did you hear what they were crying?"

Lucy was utterly amazed. She saw, in her mind's eye, all those millions of creatures, all the creepy-crawlies, clinging to stones and weeds under the water, with their mouths wide, all screeching. And the fish – she could see the dense processions of shuddering, flashing buckles and brooches, the millions of gold-ringed eyes, with their pouting lips stretched wide – screeching. And the frogs that have no lips – screaming. She suddenly remembered how the giant woman had rubbed her eyes in pain, and she thought of the wet frogs, just as wet and naked as eyeballs, burning – rubbing their eyes with their rubbery almost human fingers. And the eels – that eel. Now she knew. That eel's silent writhings had been a screaming

"What's happening?" she cried.

The Iron Woman raised her right arm and pointed at the river with her index finger. The ringing in Lucy's ears now seemed to be coming out of the end of that finger. She looked towards where the finger was pointing. The river rolled and swirled, just as before. But now it seemed that a hole had appeared in it, a fiery hole, and she could see something moving far down in the hole.

It was the eel again. Just as she had seen it before, there it was, writhing, and knotting and unknotting itself. But it was coming towards her, just as if the fiery hole were a tunnel. It came dancing and contorting itself up the bright, fiery tunnel. Now it was very close to them, in the mouth of the strange hole. She heard a crying, and knew it was the eel. And there were words in the crying. She could almost make them out, but not quite. She strained to hear the words coming from the eel that seemed to be twisting and burning in a kind of fiery furnace. And it did seem to be burning. In front of her eyes it blazed and charred, becoming a smoky, dim shape, a spinning wisp. Then the hole was empty.

But already another form had appeared far down in the fiery hole, coming towards them in a writhing dance.

It was a barbel. It danced as if it walked the water on its vibrating tail, swaying and twisting to keep its balance. Lucy could see the little tentacles of its beard lashing around its mouth as it jerked and spun in the fiery hole. And the barbel too was crying. It seemed to be shouting, or rather yelling, the same thing over and over. But still Lucy could not make out the words. And again, as she strained to catch the words, the barbel writhed into a twist of smoke and vanished, just as the eel had done. But already, far down inside the hole, she could see the next creature. And this time it was an otter.

Just like the others, the otter came twisting and tumbling towards them, up the fiery tunnel, in a writhing sort of dance, as if it were trying to escape from itself. And as it came it was crying something, just like the eel and the barbel. Again, Lucy could almost hear the words, louder and louder as it danced nearer and nearer, till it spun into a blot of smoke at the hole mouth and vanished.

After that came a kingfisher. This dazzling little bird came whirling and crying till it fluttered itself into a blaze of smoke like a firework spinning on a nail.

After that came a frog. The frog's dance was simply a leaping up and a falling down on its back. Then it scrambled to its feet, leapt up and fell on its back, over and over, as if it were inside some kind of spinning fiery bubble, inside the fiery hole. But its voice came loud and clear, a wailing cry like the same words shouted again and again. But Lucy still could not make out what words those were, till the frog too whirled into smoke.

Then came a squirming thing that Lucy could not make out. Then with a shock she recognized it. It was a human baby. It looked like a fat pink newt, jerking and flailing inside a fiery bubble. But just like those other creatures it came up the fiery tunnel, doing its dance, which was like a fighting to kick, and claw its way out of the fiery bubble. This time the crying was not like words. It was simply crying – the wailing, desperate cry of a human baby when it cries as if the world had ended.

Lucy could not bear to see any more. She knew this baby, too, would suddenly burst into flames, blaze into a whirl of smoke and vanish. She dropped her face into her hands. Her shoulders shook as she sobbed.

As she got control of herself, she suddenly thought: This is my nightmare. I'm back in it. If I make a big effort, I'll wake up and everything will be all right. And she looked up.

But if she hoped to see her attic bedroom with the case of five stuffed owls, it was no good. There in front of her eyes were the black columns of the legs of the Iron Woman. And there was the cold river. And she could feel that strangeness in her ears, that ringing, but fainter now, with the singing of the birds breaking through.

The Iron Woman was gazing out through the trees. "What's happened?" cried Lucy. "Oh, what's wrong with everything?"

The rumbling voice shook the air softly all around her. "Them," she heard, in a low thunder. "Them. Them. They have done it. And I have come to destroy them."

The great black eyes stared at Lucy – black and yet also

red, with a dull glow. Then the voice came again, louder, like a distant explosion: "Destroy them!"

And again, still louder, so the air or her ears or her whole head seemed to split. Her whole body cringed, as if a jet fighter had suddenly roared down out of nowhere ten feet above the treetops:

"Destroy them!"

Who? Lucy was wondering wildly. Who does she mean? Who are "them"? And she would have asked, but the Iron Woman had lifted a foot high above the ground and for a frightful moment Lucy thought this huge, terrible being had gone mad, like a mad elephant, and was going to stamp her flat. Then the foot came down hard, and the river bank jumped. The Iron Woman raised her other foot. She raised her arms. Her giant fists clenched and unclenched. Her foot came down and the ground leaped. Her eyes now glared bright red, like traffic lights at danger.

Slowly, the vast shape began to dance, there on the river bank. Lifting one great foot and slamming it down. Lifting the other great foot. She began to circle slowly. Her stamping sounded like deep slow drumbeats, echoing through her iron body. But as she danced, she sang, in that awful voice, as if Lucy were dangling from the tail of a jet fighter just behind the jets:

"DESTROY THE POISONERS.
THE IGNORANT ONES.
DESTROY THE POISONERS.
THE IGNORANT ONES.
THE RUBBISHERS.
DESTROY.
THE RUBBISHERS.
DESTROY."

She wasn't singing so much as roaring and groaning. She seemed to have forgotten Lucy. It was an incredible sight. The size of several big elephants rolled into one, and now working herself up, every second more and more enraged. And Lucy was thinking: She must mean the Waste Factory. People are always worrying about how the Waste Factory poisons everything. She'll trample the whole thing flat. Nothing can stop her.

Lucy's father worked at the Waste Factory. Everybody worked at the Waste Factory. Only the month before, the Waste Factory had doubled its size. It was importing waste now from all over the world. It was booming. Her father had just had another rise in wages.

At the same time, she thought of the million screams of all the water creatures, and even that human baby, inside the Iron Woman's body. No wonder she was roaring and writhing in that awful dance. All the creatures were screaming inside her, and the sound came out of her mouth as this terrible roar. Everybody within miles must be hearing it. And maybe the Iron Woman truly was going mad in front of her eyes, with the torments of all those burning, twisting, screaming water creatures inside her.

Then Lucy swayed on her feet, the darkness came rushing in from all sides, and she dropped in a faint. And she lay there unconscious, as the earth beneath her jolted and quivered.

NOAH'S ARK

THE KING JAMES BIBLE, GENESIS 6–8

A very early conservation tale, and the most famous of all. Echoes here of the global destruction we bring upon ourselves if we do not live in harmony with the world around us.

AND IT CAME TO PASS, when men began to multiply on the face of the earth, and daughters were born unto them, that the sons of God saw the daughters of men that they were fair; and they took them wives of all which they chose.

And the Lord said, My spirit shall not always strive with man, for that he also is flesh: yet his days shall be an hundred and twenty years.

There were giants in the earth in those days; and also after that, when the sons of God came in unto the daughters of men, and they bare children to them, the same became mighty men which were of old, men of renown.

And God saw that the wickedness of man was great in the earth, and that every imagination of the thoughts of his heart was only evil continually.

And it repented the Lord that he had made man on the

earth, and it grieved him at his heart.

And the Lord said, I will destroy man whom I have created from the face of the earth; both man, and beast, and the creeping thing, and the fowls of the air; for it repenteth me that I have made them.

But Noah found grace in the eyes of the Lord.

These are the generations of Noah: Noah was a just man and perfect in his generations, and Noah walked with God.

And Noah begat three sons, Shem, Ham, and Japheth.

The earth also was corrupt before God, and the earth was filled with violence.

And God looked upon the earth, and, behold, it was corrupt; for all flesh had corrupted his way upon the earth.

And God said unto Noah, The end of all flesh is come before me; for the earth is filled with violence through them; and, behold, I will destroy them with the earth.

Make thee an ark of gopher wood; rooms shalt thou make in the ark, and shalt pitch it within and without with pitch.

And this is the fashion which thou shalt make it of: The length of the ark shall be three hundred cubits, the breadth of it fifty cubits, and the height of it thirty cubits.

A window shalt thou make to the ark, and in a cubit shalt thou finish it above; and the door of the ark shalt thou set in the side thereof; with lower, second, and third stories shalt thou make it.

And, behold, I, even I, do bring a flood of waters upon the earth, to destroy all flesh, wherein is the breath of life, from under heaven; and every thing that is in the earth shall die.

But with thee I will establish my covenant; and thou shalt come into the ark, thou, and thy sons, and thy wife, and thy sons' wives with thee.

And of every living thing of all flesh, two of every sort

shalt thou bring into the ark, to keep them alive with thee; they shall be male and female.

Of fowls after their kind, and of cattle after their kind, of every creeping thing of the earth after his kind, two of every sort shall come unto thee, to keep them alive.

And take thou unto thee of all food that is eaten, and thou shalt gather it to thee; and it shall be for food for thee, and for them.

Thus did Noah; according to all that God commanded him, so did he.

And the Lord said unto Noah, Come thou and all thy house into the ark: for thee have I seen righteous before me in this generation.

Of every clean beast thou shalt take to thee by sevens, the male and his female: and of beasts that are not clean by two, the male and his female.

Of fowls also of the air by sevens, the male and the female; to keep seed alive upon the face of all the earth.

For yet seven days, and I will cause it to rain upon the earth forty days and forty nights; and every living substance that I have made will I destroy from off the face of the earth.

And Noah did according unto all that the Lord commanded him.

And Noah was six hundred years old when the flood of waters was upon the earth.

And Noah went in, and his sons, and his wife, and his sons' wives with him, into the ark, because of the waters of the flood.

Of clean beasts, and of beasts that are not clean, and of fowls, and of every thing that creepeth upon the earth, there went in two and two unto Noah into the ark, the male and the female, as God had commanded Noah.

And it came to pass after seven days, that the waters of the flood were upon the earth.

In the six hundredth year of Noah's life, in the second month, the seventeenth day of the month, the same day were all the fountains of the great deep broken up, and the windows of heaven were opened.

And the rain was upon the earth forty days and forty nights.

In the selfsame day entered Noah, and Shem, and Ham, and Japheth, the sons of Noah, and Noah's wife, and the three wives of his sons with them, into the ark; they, and every beast after his kind, and all the cattle after their kind, and every creeping thing that creepeth upon the earth after his kind, and every fowl after his kind, every bird of every sort.

And they went in unto Noah into the ark, two and two of all flesh, wherein is the breath of life.

And they that went in, went in male and female of all flesh, as God had commanded him: and the Lord shut him in.

And the flood was forty days upon the earth; and the waters increased, and bare up the ark, and it was lift up above the earth.

And the waters prevailed, and were increased greatly upon the earth; and the ark went upon the face of the waters.

And the waters prevailed exceedingly upon the earth; and all the high hills that were under the whole heaven were covered.

Fifteen cubits upward did the waters prevail; and the mountains were covered.

And all flesh died that moved upon the earth, both of fowl, and of cattle, and of beast, and of every creeping thing that creepeth upon the earth, and every man: all in whose nostrils was the breath of life, of all that was in the dry land, died.

And every living substance was destroyed which was upon the face of the ground, both man, and cattle, and the creeping things, and the fowl of the heaven; and they were destroyed from the earth: and Noah only remained alive, and they that were with him in the ark.

And the waters prevailed upon the earth an hundred and fifty days.

And God remembered Noah and every living thing, and all the cattle that was with him in the ark: and God made a wind to pass over the earth, and the waters asswaged; the fountains also of the deep and the windows of heaven were stopped, and the rain from heaven was restrained; and the waters returned from off the earth continually: and after the end of the hundred and fifty days the waters were abated.

And the ark rested in the seventh month, on the seventeenth day of the month, upon the mountains of Ararat.

And the waters decreased continually until the tenth month: in the tenth month, on the first day of the month, were the tops of the mountains seen.

And it came to pass at the end of forty days, that Noah opened the window of the ark which he had made: and he sent forth a raven, which went forth to and fro, until the waters were dried up from off the earth.

Also he sent forth a dove from him, to see if the waters were abated from off the face of the ground; but the dove found no rest for the sole of her foot, and she returned unto him into the ark, for the waters were on the face of the whole earth: then he put forth his hand, and took her, and pulled her in unto him into the ark.

And he stayed yet other seven days; and again he sent forth the dove out of the ark; and the dove came in to him in the evening; and, lo, in her mouth was an olive leaf pluckt off: so Noah knew that the waters were abated from off the earth.

And he stayed yet other seven days; and sent forth the dove; which returned not again unto him any more.

And it came to pass in the six hundredth and first year, in the first month, the first day of the month, the waters were dried up from off the earth: and Noah removed the covering of the ark, and looked, and, behold, the face of the ground was dry.

And in the second month, on the seven and twentieth of the month, was the earth dried.

And God spake unto Noah, saying, Go forth of the ark, thou, and thy wife, and thy sons, and thy sons' wives with thee.

Bring forth with thee every living thing that is with thee, of all flesh, both of fowl, and of cattle, and of every creeping thing that creepeth upon the earth; that they may breed abundantly in the earth, and be fruitful, and multiply upon the earth.

And Noah went forth, and his sons, and his wife, and his sons' wives with him: every beast, every creeping thing, and every fowl, and whatsoever creepeth on the earth, after their kinds, went forth out of the ark.

And Noah builded an altar unto the Lord; and took of every clean beast, and took of every clean fowl, and offered burnt offerings on the altar.

And the Lord smelled a sweet savour; and the Lord said in his heart, I will not again curse the ground any more for man's sake; for the imagination of man's heart is evil from his youth; neither will I again smite any more every thing living, as I have done.

While the earth remaineth, seedtime and harvest, and cold and heat, and summer and winter, and day and night shall not cease.

THE VOYAGE OF THE *BEAGLE*

CHARLES DARWIN

Darwin's five-year scientific survey of the coasts and interiors from South America to the South Sea Islands on HMS Beagle *began in 1831. His observations as a naturalist were to change entirely the way we think of ourselves and our origins. Published in 1839, and written as a journal, this is a true tale of never-to-be-forgotten adventures, of wonderful encounters with animals of all kinds – but written always as a scientist, closely observed and meticulously recorded.*

OCTOBER 8TH – We arrived at James Island; this island, as well as Charles Island, were long since thus named after our kings of the Stuart line. Mr Bynoe, myself, and our servants were left here for a week, with provisions and a tent, whilst the *Beagle* went for water. We found here a party of Spaniards, who had been sent from Charles Island to dry fish, and to salt tortoise-meat. About six miles inland, and at the height of nearly 2000 feet, a hovel had been built in which two men lived, who were employed in catching tortoises, whilst the others were fishing on the coast. I paid this party two visits, and slept there one night. As in the other islands, the lower region was covered by nearly leafless bushes, but the trees were here of a larger growth than elsewhere, several being two feet and some even two feet nine inches in diameter. The upper region being kept damp by the clouds, supports a green and flourishing vegetation. So damp was the ground, that there were large beds of a coarse cyperus, in which great numbers of a very small water-rail lived and bred. While staying in this upper region, we lived entirely on tortoise-meat: the breastplate roasted (as the gauchos do *carne con cuero*), with the flesh on it, is very good; and the young tortoises make excellent soup; but otherwise the meat to my taste is indifferent.

One day we accompanied a party of the Spaniards in their whale-boat to a salina, or lake from which salt is procured. After landing, we had a very rough walk over a rugged field of recent lava, which has almost surrounded a tuff-crater, at the bottom of which the salt-lake lies. The water is only three or four inches deep, and rests on a layer of beautifully crystallized, white salt. The lake is quite circular, and is fringed with a border of bright green succulent plants; the almost precipitous walls of the crater are clothed with wood, so that the scene was altogether both picturesque and curious. A few years since, the sailors belonging to a sealing-vessel murdered their captain in this quiet spot; and we saw his skull lying among the bushes.

During the greater part of our stay of a week, the sky was cloudless, and if the trade-wind failed for an hour, the heat became very oppressive. On two days, the thermometer within the tent stood for some hours at 93°; but in the open air, in the wind and sun, at only 85°. The sand was extremely hot; the thermometer placed in some of a brown colour immediately rose to 137°, and how much above that it would have risen, I do not know, for it was not graduated any higher. The black sand felt much hotter, so that even in thick boots it was quite disagreeable to walk over it.

The natural history of these islands is eminently curious, and well deserves attention. Most of the organic productions are aboriginal creations, found nowhere else; there is even a difference between the inhabitants of the different islands; yet all show a marked relationship with those of America, though separated from that continent by an open space of ocean, between 500 and 600 miles in width. The archipelago is a little world within itself, or rather a satellite attached to America, whence it has derived a few stray colonists, and has received the general character of its indigenous productions. Considering the small size of these islands, we feel the more astonished at the number of their aboriginal beings, and at their confined range. Seeing every height crowned with its crater, and the boundaries of most of the lava-streams still distinct, we are led to believe that within a period, geologically recent, the unbroken ocean was here spread out. Hence, both in space and time, we seem to be brought somewhat near to that great fact – that mystery of mysteries – the first appearance of new beings on this earth.

Of terrestrial mammals, there is only one which must be considered as indigenous, namely, a mouse (*Mus galapagoensis*), and this is confined, as far as I could ascertain, to Chatham Island, the most easterly island of the group. It belongs, as I am informed by Mr Waterhouse, to a division of the family of mice characteristic of America. At James Island, there is a rat sufficiently distinct from the common kind to have been named and described by Mr Waterhouse; but as it belongs to the old-world division of the family, and as this island has been frequented by ships for the last hundred and fifty years, I can hardly doubt that this rat is merely a variety, produced by the new and peculiar climate, food and soil, to which it has been subjected. Although no one has a right to speculate without distinct facts, yet even with respect to the Chatham Island mouse, it should be borne in mind, that it may possibly be an American species imported here; for I have seen, in a most unfrequented part of the pampas, a native mouse living in the roof of a newly-built hovel, and therefore its transportation in a vessel is not improbable: analogous facts have been observed by Dr Richardson in North America.

We will now turn to the order of reptiles, which gives the most striking character to the zoology of these islands. The species are not numerous, but the numbers of individuals of each species are extraordinarily great. There is one small lizard belonging to a South American genus, and two species (and probably more) of the *Amblyrhynchus* – a genus confined to the Galapagos islands. There is one snake which is numerous; it is identical, as I am informed by M. Bibron, with the *Psammophis temminckii* from Chile. Of sea-turtle I believe there is more than one species; and of tortoises there are, as we shall presently show, two or three species or races. Of toads and frogs there are none: I was surprised at this, considering how well suited for them the temperate and damp upper woods appeared to be. It recalled to my mind the remark made by Bory St Vincent, namely, that none of this family are found on any of the volcanic islands in the great oceans. As far as I can ascertain from various works, this seems to hold good throughout the Pacific, and even in the large islands of the Sandwich archipelago. Mauritius offers an apparent exception, where I saw the *Rana mascariensis* in abundance: this frog is said now to inhabit the Seychelles, Madagascar, and Bourbon; but on the other hand, Du Bois, in his voyage of 1669, states that there were no reptiles in Bourbon except tortoises; and the Officier du Roi asserts that before 1768 it had been attempted, without success, to introduce frogs into Mauritius – I presume, for the purpose of eating: hence it may be well doubted whether this frog is an aboriginal of these islands. The absence of the frog family in the oceanic islands is the more remarkable, when contrasted with the case of lizards, which swarm on most of the smallest islands. May this difference not be caused, by the greater facility with which the eggs of lizards, protected by calcareous shells, might be transported through salt-water, than could the slimy spawn of frog?

I will first describe the habits of the tortoise (*Testudo nigra*, formerly called *indica*), which has been so frequently alluded to. These animals are found, I believe, on all the islands of the archipelago; certainly on the greater number. They frequent in preference the high damp parts, but they likewise live in the lower and arid districts. I have already shown, from the numbers which have been caught in a single day, how very numerous they must be. Some grow to an immense size: Mr Lawson, an Englishman, and vice-governor of the colony, told us that he had seen several so large, that it required six or eight men to lift them from the ground; and that some had afforded as much as 200 pounds of meat. The old males are the largest, the females rarely growing to so great a size: the male can readily be distinguished from the female by the greater length of its tail. The tortoises which live on those islands where there is no water, or in the lower and arid parts of the others, feed chiefly on the succulent cactus. Those which frequent the higher and damp regions, eat the leaves of various trees, a kind of berry (called *guayavita*) which is acid and austere, and likewise a pale green filamentous lichen (*Usnera plicata*), that hangs in tresses from the boughs of the trees.

The tortoise is very fond of water, drinking large quantities, and wallowing in the mud. The larger islands alone possess springs, and these are always situated towards the central parts, and at a considerable height. The tortoises, therefore, which frequent the lower districts, when thirsty are obliged to travel from a long distance. Hence broad and well-beaten paths branch off in every direction from the wells down to the sea-coast; and the Spaniards by following them up, first discovered the watering-places. When I landed at Chatham Island, I could not imagine what animal travelled so methodically along well-chosen tracks. Near the springs it was a curious spectacle to behold many of these huge creatures, one set eagerly travelling onwards with outstretched necks, and another set returning, after having drunk their fill. When the tortoise arrives at the spring, quite regardless of any spectator, he buries his head in the water above his eyes, and greedily swallows great mouthfuls, at the rate of about ten in a minute. The inhabitants say each animal stays three or four days in the neighbourhood of the water, and then returns to the lower country; but they differed respecting the frequency of these visits. The animal probably regulates them according to the nature of the food on which it has lived. It is, however, certain, that tortoises can subsist even on those islands, where there is no other water than what falls during a few rainy days in the year.

I believe it is well ascertained, that the bladder of the frog acts as a reservoir for the moisture necessary to its existence: such seems to be the case with the tortoise. For some time after a visit to the springs, their urinary bladders are distended with fluid, which is said gradually to decrease in volume, and to become less pure. The inhabitants, when walking in the lower district, and overcome with thirst, often take advantage of this circumstance, and drink the contents of the bladder if full: in one I saw killed, the fluid was quite limpid, and had only a very slightly bitter taste. The inhabitants, however, always first drink the water in the pericardium, which is described as being best.

The tortoises, when purposely moving towards any point, travel by night and day, and arrive at their journey's end much sooner than would be expected. The inhabitants, from observing marked individuals, consider that they travel a distance of about eight miles in two or three days. One large tortoise, which I watched, walked at the rate of sixty yards in ten minutes, that is 360 yards in the hour, or four miles a day – allowing a little time for it to eat on the road. During the breeding season, when the male and female are together, the male utters a hoarse roar or bellowing, which, it is said, can be heard at the distance of more than a hundred yards. The female never uses her voice, and the male only at these times; so that when the people hear this noise, they know that the two are together. They were at this time (October) laying their eggs. The female, where the soil is sandy, deposits them together, and covers them up with sand; but where the ground is rocky she drops them indiscriminately in any hole: Mr Bynoe found seven placed in a fissure. The egg is white and spherical; one which I measured was seven inches and three-eighths in circumference, and therefore larger than a hen's egg. The young tortoises, as soon as they are hatched, fall a prey in great numbers to the carrion-feeding buzzard. The old ones seem generally to die from accidents, as from falling down precipices: at least, several of the inhabitants told

me, that they had never found one dead without some evident cause.

The inhabitants believe that these animals are absolutely deaf; certainly they do not overhear a person walking close behind them. I was always amused when overtaking one of these great monsters, as it was quietly pacing along, to see how suddenly, the instant I passed, it would draw in its head and legs, and uttering a deep hiss fall to the ground with a heavy sound, as if struck dead. I frequently got on their backs, and then giving a few raps on the hinder part of their shells, they would rise up and walk away – but I found it very difficult to keep my balance. The flesh of this animal is largely employed, both fresh and salted; and a beautiful clear oil is prepared from the fat. When a tortoise is caught, the man makes a slit in the skin near its tail, so as to see inside its body, whether the fat under the dorsal plate is thick. If it is not, the animal is liberated; and it is said to recover soon from this strange operation. In order to secure the tortoises, it is not sufficient to turn them like turtle, for they are often able to get on their legs again.

There can be little doubt that this tortoise is an aboriginal inhabitant of the Galapagos; for it is found on all, or nearly all, the islands, even on some of the smaller ones where there is no water; had it been an imported species, this would hardly have been the case in a group which has been so little frequented. Moreover, the old buccaneers found this tortoise in greater numbers even than at present: Wood and Rogers also, in 1708, say that it is the opinion of the Spaniards, that it is found nowhere else in this quarter of the world. It is now widely distributed; but it may be questioned whether it is in any other place aboriginal. The bones of a tortoise at Mauritius, associated with those of the extinct dodo, have generally been considered as belonging to this tortoise: if this had been so, undoubtedly it must have been there indigenous; but M. Bibron informs me that he believes that it was distinct, as the species now living there certainly is.

* * *

From just such observations, Darwin went on to develop his theory of evolution by natural selection, which he put forward in The Origin of Species, *published in 1859.*

WOLF BROTHER

CHIEF BUFFALO CHILD LONG LANCE

Chief Buffalo Child Long Lance was born in the early 1880s. He was a boxer, a wrestler, a soldier in the First World War, and a writer. Here he provides an insight into how it was when men lived close to the animal world – so close they felt as one with their fellow creatures. There have been moments in the countryside when I have genuinely felt that closeness. They are moments of the purest pleasure.

FOLLOWING THIS TERRIBLE BATTLE with the Crees, our chiefs decided that we should pick some quiet place in the Rockies and spend the remainder of the winter there. There were large herds of Wild Horses running the ranges of the big plateau between the Cascades and the Rocky Mountains – Northern British Columbia – and our fathers decided that we should stay here until spring came, and then go west to this plateau and capture a herd of good Horses, before venturing out on to the plains again.

We travelled northwestward through the mountains until we came to the western foothills of the Rockies, and here in a deep snow-covered pocket of the Rockies we settled down for the remainder of the winter.

In our band at that time we had a very noted warrior and hunter named Eagle Plume. It was the custom in those days, when the men were being killed so often and the women were growing to outnumber them, for one warrior to have from three to five wives. It was the only way that we could make sure that all of our women would be taken care of when they should reach old age.

But this warrior, Eagle Plume, had only one wife. He was a tall, handsome warrior of vigorous middle age, and but for one thing he was well contented with his pretty wife. She had served him well. She was always busy preparing his meals and waiting upon him; and tanning the hides of the furry denizens of the wilderness, which were killed in large numbers by this famous hunter of the Blackfeet. But she had no children.

Indians are extremely fond of children, and to have no offspring is regarded as a calamity, a curse. Boy children were always preferred; as they could grow up to be hunters and warriors, while girl children could be of little economic use to the family or the tribe.

Eagle Plume thought of adding another wife to his camp, one who might bear him a child; but he loved his faithful young woman and he was reluctant to put this idea into execution. He was unlike many men; he could love but one woman.

However, children were wanted, and Eagle Plume's wife had spent many hours crying alone in her tepee, because the Great Spirit had not given her the power to present him with a baby with which to make their life complete. We heard our old people discuss this, and many times they would send us over to Eagle Plume's camp to play and to keep them company. They would treat us like their own children and give us attentions which we would not receive even from our own parents.

Like all great Indian hunters, Eagle Plume liked most to hunt alone. As we camped in the Northern Rockies that winter, he would go out by himself and remain for days. He would return heavily laden with the pelts of Otter, Mink, Black Wolf, Marten, and Lynx.

It was well through the winter toward spring, and the snow was still very deep, when early one morning he set out on one of his periodic hunting trips into the wild country to the north of where we were camping. That evening as he was making his way down a mountain draw to seek out a campsite, a Wolf came out of the bush and howled at him in the bitter white twilight.

It was a big Wolf, not a Coyote, but one of the largest specimens of the huge black Timber-wolf. With the true curiosity of the Wolf, it watched Eagle Plume make camp, then it went quietly away.

"Go now, my brother," said Eagle Plume. "Tomorrow, I will follow you for that thick fur on your skin."

And so the next morning, running on his snowshoes, and with a large round ball in his muzzle-loader, Eagle Plume went on the trail of the Wolf.

It was easy for an Indian to follow its path, because its tracks were bigger than any Wolf tracks he had ever seen. It led Eagle Plume a far journey across a hanging mountain valley and on through a heavily forested range of low-lying mountains. The Wolf seemed to be bent steadily on a trail that led due north. Nothing, not even the fresh cross-trails of Caribou, had swerved it from this purposeful course. It acted not like a hunted thing evading its pursuer.

Eagle Plume had travelled all day, and the late afternoon sun was making long shadows, when suddenly as he peered ahead, he saw the big Wolf run out on a naked ridge that rolled up from a bushy mountain plain.

It had been snowing for some hours in a quiet, intense

way; and with the descent of the sun, the wind was rising with fitful whines, making little swirling gusts of snow-drift on the white surface of the land, which foretold the approach of a mountain storm. The new snow had made the going heavy for Eagle Plume, and it must have been tiring to the Wolf, too; for it was now sinking to its belly with each step.

Eagle Plume was a tireless hunter, and he knew that if the Wolf kept to the open country, he, with the superiority of his snowshoes, could wear it down. Already the big, shaggy creature was showing signs of fatigue, and the intrepid hunter was remorselessly closing up the distance that his quarry was losing.

After his first view of the Wolf on the ridge, Eagle Plume lost sight of it for a while; then he saw it again, and when the sun, with its sinister attendants of two false suns, touched the rim of the mountains to the west, the Wolf remained in plain view all of the time. The Blackfoot was sweeping forward on the bumpy surface of the great rolling sea of snow at a long, tireless lope, while the Wolf seemed to be floundering along in distress.

The wind continued to rise, and soon the country was enveloped in a stinging, blinding chaos of drifting snow. A blizzard was coming up. And even the Wolf, wild denizen of the region as he was, was now seeking harbourage.

The mountain valley lay flat and expressionless under its snowy mantle. The only relief to the landscape was a pine grove which stood like an island straight ahead.

A blizzard had no terrors for a good hunter like Eagle Plume, when there was wood and shelter in sight. He knew that the Wolf was making for cover, and he hurried his footsteps so that he might overtake it and make his kill before it escaped into the pines or became lost in the darkness of the raging blizzard.

But the storm gathered in strength and violence, and Eagle Plume was forced to summon all of his remaining energies to reach the shelter of the trees before darkness and death should overtake him. When, panting and exhausted, he at last made his objective, he had long since lost sight and track of his game.

He rested briefly and then began to skirt the lea side of the pines for a suitable place to make fire and camp. As he was doing this, he suddenly became aware that the Wolf was watching him from a nearby snowbank. Cautiously he turned in his tracks and levelled the long, cold barrel of his gun straight between a pair of furtive grey eyes – wild, slanted eyes, which looked calmly at him like two pieces of grey flint. He paused for a second and then pulled the trigger. There was a flash in the nipple – but no explosion. The priming had been affected by the drifting snow.

With his teeth he pulled the wooden stopper of his powder-horn and poured dry powder into the pan, keeping his eyes on the steady gaze of the Wolf, which made no effort to move or escape. As he deftly reloaded and primed his gun, he spoke softly to the Wolf in the manner of the Indian, saying:

"Oh, my brother, I will not keep you waiting in the cold and snow, I am preparing the messenger I will send you. Have patience for just a little while."

As he shook the dry powder on to the pan of his gun, the Wolf, without any previous movement of warning, suddenly made a mighty leap – and vanished.

The swift-gathering darkness and the howling blizzard made useless any further effort to capture this remarkable pelt, and realizing for the first time the futility of his quest, Eagle Plume now laid aside his gun and unloosened an axe which hung at his belt, and made hurried preparations to shield himself from the blizzard. He cut down some dead spruce for a fire, and then made himself a shelter of mountain bushes.

During a slight pause in his labour, his ear, keenly attuned to the voices of the wilderness, caught a strange sound. When he listened intently and caught it a second time there was no mistaking what it was. It was the wail of a child.

Throwing down his axe and wrapping his blanket about his head and body, he stumbled out into the darkness and hurried blindly into the direction whence the wail had come. As he jogged along through the swirling snow, his ears alert to hold the wailing sound above that of the screeching wind, one of his snowshoes caught in something and he fell face-forward into the snow. As he got up and reached down to pick up his blanket, his hand touched the heavy object which had tripped him. He kneeled down and looked at it – and it was a woman – an Indian woman – a dead Indian woman.

Still the wailing continued. He walked around and around trying to locate it. It seemed to come from the air, not from the ground. From point to point he walked and stopped and listened. Finally he walked up to a tree, and there, hanging high out of the reach of prowling animals, he found a living child in a moss bag – a baby a few months old.

Snug in its native cradle, packed with dry moss and Rabbit skins, it had suffered none from the cold.

He built a great fire and made a camp, and slept that night with the foundling wrapped in his arms.

In the morning he snared some Rabbits, and slitting the throat of one with his hunting knife, he pressed the warm blood into the mouth of the hungry infant.

With his axe and some saplings it did not take him long to knock together a rough sleigh. And so he came back to our camp in the valley, dragging the unknown dead woman behind him; and underneath his capote he carried the child in its moss bag.

When the people of our camp came out to meet this strange company of two living and one dead, he handed the baby to his wife and said:

"Here is our child; we will no longer have need for a strange woman in our lodge."

Eagle Plume's wife cradled the child in her arms and warmed it to her bosom; and our old people said that the fires of maternity kindled in her at the touch of the infant, and that milk for its sustenance flowed in those breasts that for so long had been dry.

That night as we sat around the campfire and Eagle Plume told his story with all the graphic detail of an Indian recital, a big Wolf cried its deep-throated howl from a high butte that overlooked our camp.

"*Mokuyi!* – It is he, the Wolf!" cried Eagle Plume. Then, raising his hand, he declared: "I shall never kill another; they are my brothers."

And, on the instant he turned to the child and christened him, Mokuyi-Oskon, Wolf Brother, and he was known by this name until he was eighteen.

The child grew and flourished. He became a great chief; and his name is today graven on a stone shaft which commemorates the termination of intertribal Indian wars in the Northwest.

SON-SON FETCHES THE MULE

JAMES BERRY

I have noticed on our farm how animals often seem to empathize with children. The horse, the donkey, the goose, the cow – all know they have nothing to fear from a child. Sometimes though, as in this story set in Jamaica, empathy needs a little encouragement.

ANIMALS HAVE ANOTHER SENSE, it would seem. They know when you are a child, and they love you for being a child. An animal will let a child pet him, boss him and even handle him upside-down, in any crazy or awkward old way, like he was dead. He would love it and give himself up to it, limply and totally. But there are other times when an animal hates it if a boy gets the better of him. That happened to Son-Son. Just fetching the mule, Son-Son found himself in trouble with him. Not expecting it, the good-good behaviour of the work mule was all spite, all vicious teeth and hooves kicked up in the air. And now Son-Son had the mule to fetch as a regular morning job, before school.

Yesterday – first time he started this new job – the mule gave him a really bad time. He played bad man. Could have damaged him! And nobody must ever know – *must ever know* – he couldn't handle Maroontugger, couldn't deal with him. Son-Son knew it and saw it: this job was his job. He must do it himself.

Like yesterday, today was an everyday warm tropical early morning. Son-Son carried a coil of rope over his shoulder. His dad had told him to carry it. He should use the rope to make a halter around Maroontugger's head, before he untethered him.

Son-Son came alone into the field of high grass. Much more excited than worried, he felt good. And he looked good. He wore his long-peaked white cap, short-sleeved floral shirt, short trousers and his sandals. He walked under one of the coconut-palm trees that stood scattered about. Even when his sandals and toes quickly got wet with dew from the grass and weeds he didn't mind. Son-Son took no notice of the morning sunlight or the tree shadows. He took no notice of noisy birds fluttering in trees, doing peep-peeps, squawk-squawks, coo-coos or just straight singing. Son-Son's job made him walk nippily on, eyes ahead. Everything about him made him look purposeful.

In truth, Son-Son was thinking he liked the business of helping his dad. It made him feel grown-up. But, best, really, it was great to handle and ride the big mule totally on his own. He'd handled Maroontugger before, lots of times, though not by himself, till yesterday. They knew each other well. Yet when he came to take Maroontugger in for work yesterday, the mule treated him like a stranger. The mule put on a bad-bad face. Tried to attack him! He had to jump quick, away from the mule's kicks! And he wouldn't let him get the loop of rope round his long head; he wouldn't let him get on his back to ride him home; then he kicked-up and kicked-up, trying to throw him off.

At one time yesterday he'd gotten worried his job was taking him too long. And he'd figured it out that the mule didn't at all like a ten year old taking him in for work. Then he'd also seen that it wasn't anything about *him* that Maroontugger disliked. The mule worked too hard. And, after all, who could blame him trying to get a day off? But a job was a job. He had to show Maroontugger that he had a job to do, just as he, Son-Son, had a job to do as well. And bad and vicious as the mule was, he had to take him in for work.

Son-Son came on into the field lit with morning sunlight. He saw Maroontugger. He was still feeding – head down in the field of high grass and scattered trees. Son-Son stopped. He watched the mule. He saw Maroontugger and yesterday's terrible mule-madness went from him. Evaporated! Son-Son felt good. It was great to be there alone with this big elephant-looking reddish fellow. He listened to the mule's greedy and noisy chewing. The huge jaws with half-circles of axe-like grabber teeth chewed grass again and again. The working of the big jaws made a noise like a grinding in an empty barrel. Son-Son's eyes widened and shone. "Jees!" he thought. "Terrific! Terrific how the grinding of the strong and loud eating has no good manners! No good manners at all!"

In his friendliest voice, Son-Son said, "Good mornin', Maroontug! Good mornin'!"

The mule lifted his head, tossed his long ears forward and stopped chewing. His steady eyes watched Son-Son. And Son-Son couldn't guess that in the straight look the mule said, "Oh! So that's it! It's you again. The boss sent you again. You the boy to take me in for work! Well, we'll see! We'll see about that, won't we?"

Son-Son grinned. "Ahright, Maroontugger? Between we, you an' me the tops, you know! Ahright?" The mule's long ears, tossed forward over his eyes, reminded him of his own long-peaked cap on his head. He walked forward. "Had a good night, Tugger-boy? Sleeping alone under stars?" Son-Son stopped again, looking round, fascinated as he had been the morning before. The high grass had been eaten or trampled down in a circle, as much as the mule's rope would allow. Son-Son said, "So you eat an' eat all through the night! No sleep, then? You just eat an' eat right through till daylight? Gosh! I couldn't do that. I couldn't eat all night like that, Tugger-boy." He looked at the mule's huge bulge of two-sided belly. "Look at your belly! Jees! Look at you! I bet you the greediest an' strongest mule, ever. I bet you could pull away any great-house. And could run away pulling any bus-load of people! Or any high-up loaded banana-truck! Listen, listen, Maroontug! I just get a great new idea.

"Everyday's always so, so sunny an' hot. Suppose one day – one day – when it really raining hard, I take you fo' a wet gallop, an' you take me fo' the wet-wet ride? Eh? How about that? Roun' an' roun' the big pasture land fo' a good wet rainy gallop, when the two of we soak-soak to the skin, dripping? Eh? Naw? Dohn like it? Okay. I think again.

"You always working. An' I always going school. Suppose, one day – one day – I dohn go school an' you dohn go work, an' we just team up? We team up big-big. We go cricket match. You walk beside me. We walk like man an' man. No rope on your head or anything. An' then, we stand together an' watch play-ball. Just watch! An' I explain the whole game to you. Then, then, when I have my best-best favourite thing – which is my barbeque jerk pork an' dry bread – I get you some sugar. Naw? No good? Well – when I have my second best-best favourite thing – which is fried fish and fried dumplin', followed by cool, ginger beer – I get you a pint-a stout. Naw? I can see you would-a like rum. Noh. No rum. I cahn buy rum like that. But – all the same – Maroontug, I got to go to school. An' you got-to go work. An' I must take you in. So, I better."

The mule stood there all the time, staring. Son-Son walked up to him, taking the coil of rope from his shoulder. He reached up to put the rope round its head and the mule's rebellion again was on. The meanest, wildest attacking look came over the mule's face. It flattened its ears back against its head. A swift dread in Son-Son's face said, stop it! stop it! as the mule swung round and kicked out at Son-Son. Only swift evasive movement saved him. But mud from the mule's iron shoes had flown up to his cheek and stuck. The mule trotted off, turned its back and stood at the full stretch of its rope, looking away.

Really cross, Son-Son was brisk. Wiping the soft blob of earth and grass from his cheek, he rushed up to the mule's face and shouted. "Maroontugger! What you think you playing at? Eh? What you think you doing? You think you all wild, stupid, bad and fool-fool! Why you behaving like you have no training? An' no respect? You want a good friend get rough an' careless with you? You wahn me beat you? You wahn feel my whip hand? I tell you – dohn change me. You well know, you a good trained worker. An' I Son-Son," tapping his chest with his fingers, "I the man who must take you in. Take you in fo' work. This very mornin'. Understan'? Ahright? So no more wild foolishness! You hear me? Good. I going put the rope round your head, softly, softly. Know that. So, easy now. Easy . . . Steady now, boy . . . Steady. Easy now . . ."

As Son-Son again was about to slip the wide loop of rope over Maroontugger's head, the mule bared his enormous teeth and clapped his jaws together near Son-Son's face. Horror-struck, "Stop et!" he bawled. His screaming rage echoed through the field and panicked the mule. It tossed its head in the air, backed off, turned round and walked away. Again it stood with its rear end turned on Son-Son, as if to say, "Go away. I don't want to see you. Don'y want anybody collecting me. Don't want any work. Sweating, sweating, all day, pulling logs uphill, pulling, pulling . . ."

Son-Son felt upset and looked it. It hurt him that Maroontugger didn't take him as a friend. "How can he not take me as a friend?" he whispered. He looked out up and down along the track at the side of the land. He stood still in the grassy field. If his dad came after him there'd be trouble. His dad knew he'd handled Maroontugger before. He might forget it was never by himself – except yesterday. It would be hard to make his dad believe Maroontugger wanted to hurt or scare him off. And – he had other morning jobs to do.

Unexpectedly, Son-Son felt better. He knew – he just knew – it wasn't himself Maroontugger disliked. For sure, it was hard work the mule wanted a rest from. True-true, the mule's job was sweaty, terrible. Two other mules tugged and pulled timber logs up to the sawmill with Maroontugger. Even so, cutting up the hillside was neither fun nor easy game to play. And whether his dad worked Maroontugger himself or not, the mule went uphill-downhill, all day long in the hot-hot sun.

His dad never took things easy himself. His dad gave way to nothing. His dad worked himself as hard as he worked his mule. Partner to another man using the electric saw, he ripped and ripped massive tree trunks into timber. By himself with a hand-saw, axe or machete, he cut and chopped away the tree limbs and branches. He cleared away branches and heaved logs. At sundown when he and Maroontugger came home each night, his dad's clothes were full of hot-sun smell and sweat and woodsap. And when he changed clothes, sawdust fell off his shirt and out of his turnups and boots.

Son-Son began to imagine everybody else getting on with their morning jobs at his yard. He imagined his mum at the paraffin stove getting breakfast. His oldest brother had fed the chickens and now fed the pigs. His sister tidied the house. His smaller brother had got the barrel more than half full with water from the standing-pipe on the village road. His dad had milked the cow. His dad would soon be sitting on the back steps sharpening his axe and machete. First to have breakfast, his dad could be having it any time now, giving half of it to the dog, Judoboy. All that meant he'd soon be ready to saddle up Maroontugger. He would soon want to wrap and sheath his machete and axe and then fasten them against the saddle, before he rode out of the yard with Judoboy following.

Unexpectedly, Son-Son head a voice, "Havin' a spot a trouble, Son-Son, mi boy?"

Son-Son swung his head round quickly and saw Mister G. He was a short man in straw hat, short sleeves and sandals, carrying a bag round his shoulder and a machete in his hand. On his way to his plot of land, Mister G had come down the lane.

"Maroontugger trying play bad-man with me, sir."

Mister G chuckled. "Yeh, I see that." He stood. He and the mule looked at each other. "Son-Son, do you job. Go right on, Son-Son. Handle him!" Mister G watched. Then he strolled away.

Son-Son began walking up to the mule. He had a new feeling. He always knew he was the mule's boss. But, now, unexpectedly, that feeling had grown much bigger. A big and bold confidence came more and more into his steps and whole body. It flowed in him like a strange magic light. The mule looked away and stood quietly, peacefully. The fearless feeling Son-Son had was terrific. He knew he had grown taller, into something almost as muscular and strong and tough as his dad. He knew this new light in him subdued the mule. He knew Maroontugger couldn't move and wouldn't move.

The mule just stood there, calm-calm, letting himself be handled. "Tuggerboy? You see how it easy? See how it easy-easy? Nice an' easy?" Son-Son had put the big loop of rope round Maroontugger's head. He then brought it against each side of the face, all the way down to the corners of the mouth. He tied the dangling rope on one side, took it across above the nose, tied it, drew a long loop for reins and tied it the other side of the mule's jaw. All the time, Son-Son looked like a midget harnessing an elephant. He completed the halter-making, feeling good. He stroked Maroontugger's neck. "You see is ahright. Ahright an' easy? Eh? Ahright an' easy? Good boy."

Son-Son led the mule to the post in the ground where he was tethered. He loosed the rope.

Son-Son really thought his battles with Maroontugger were all over. But, Maroontugger knew differently. Maroontugger's head kept a lot more secret spite to force Son-Son to leave him alone. As Son-Son tried to get up on to the mule's back the new tricks started. Every time Son-Son tried to clamber up, Maroontugger gently eased himself away like a sideways dance. And Son-Son came down again, right on his own two legs. Over and over, holding on to the rope-reins against the mule's shoulder, Son-Son heaved himself up; and each time, that smart sideways movement made him miss his mount and come down again. Finally, Son-Son chuckled with a sigh, saying "Tugger-boy – okay. You've had your go. Now I'll have mine."

Son-Son led the mule and tied his head close against a coconut tree. Then, holding the end of the rope, he climbed up the tree trunk and lowered himself down on the mule's back. Son-Son thought at last he'd won; he couldn't believe the mule kept an extra reserve store of badness saved up. The moment Son-Son drew that slippery knot he'd tied round the tree and loosed the mule, that was it! Maroontugger tugged his head, swished his tail and jumped off, racing away like a wild bull, all crazy and malicious. The mule bolted on, going its own way, without control. Son-Son could not check him. Bobbing his head with a stubborn defiance, Maroontugger raced on, going deeper into the field. He galloped recklessly under trees, trying to knock his rider off. Son-Son ducked under branches, lying down on the mule's bare back, like a North American Indian rider. His cap blew away. All the time now, he pulled and jerked and tugged at the mule's head as hard as he could, shouting, "Whoa! Whoa, now! Whoa, Maroontugger! Whoa, boy!"

At last, pulling and holding him firmly now, Son-Son turned Maroontugger round and held him to a walking pace. Not even allowed to break into a trot, he was ridden right back across the field out on to the track and then the village road.

Son-Son rode home into his yard on the big mule. He dismounted and tethered him, to await saddling up by his dad. The smell of brewed coffee, fried fish and breadfruit roasting on the woodfire made Son-Son realize how hungry he was.

He went into the kitchen and couldn't believe how everything was normal. And nobody said anything about taking too long fetching the mule. Nobody even mentioned he'd lost his cap. And he certainly would say nothing about it.

Nobody was ever going to say he couldn't manage Maroontugger. Nobody was even going to know the mule gave him a hard time. Yet, as he ate breakfast, Son-Son knew the struggle with Maroontugger wasn't over. But, he was ready. He was ready. Always, he was going to let that mule understand – Son-Son was tall-tall.

HE WAS A GOOD LION

BERYL MARKHAM

Beryl Markham was born in 1902 and grew up on a farm in East Africa. As an adult she was the first pilot to fly solo across the Atlantic, east to west. Her life reads like a novel – but then the best of fiction rings true. This story is true *and reads like the best of fiction: the story of a tame lion whose instincts get the better of him, just once.*

WHEN I WAS A CHILD, I spent all my days with the Nandi Murani, hunting barefooted, in the Rongai Valley, or in the cedar forests of the Mau Escarpment.

At first I was not permitted to carry a spear, but the Murani depended on nothing else.

You cannot hunt an animal with such a weapon unless you know the way of his life. You must know the things he loves, the things he fears, the paths he will follow. You must be sure of the quality of his speed and the measure of his courage. He will know as much about you, and at times make better use of it.

But my Murani friends were patient with me.

"*Amin yut!*" one would say, "what but a dik-dik will run like that? Your eyes are filled with clouds today, Lakweit!"

That day my eyes were filled with clouds, but they were young enough eyes and they soon cleared. There were other days and other dik-dik. There were so many things.

There were dik-dik and leopard, kongoni and warthog, buffalo, lion, and the hare that jumps. There were many thousands of the hare that jumps.

And there were wildebeest and antelope. There was the snake that crawls and the snake that climbs. There were the birds and young men like whips of leather, like rainshafts in the sun, like spears before a singiri.

"*Amin yut!*" the young men would say, "that is no buffalo spoor, Lakweit. Here! Bend down and look. Bend down and look at this mark. See how this leaf is crushed. Feel the wetness of this dung. Bend down and look so that you may learn!"

And so, in time, I learned. But some things I learned alone.

There was a place called Elkington's Farm by Kabete Station. It was near Nairobi on the edge of the Kikuyu Reserve, and my father and I used to ride there from town on horses or in a buggy, and along the way my father would tell me things about Africa.

Sometimes he would tell me stories about the tribal wars – wars between the Masai and the Kikuyu (which the Masai always won), or between the Masai and the Nandi (which neither of them ever won), and about their great leaders and their wild way of life which, to me, seemed much greater fun than our own. He would tell me of Lenana, the brilliant Masai *ol-oiboni*, who prophesied the coming of the White Man, and of Lenana's tricks and stratagems and victories, and about how his people were unconquerable and unconquered – until, in retaliation against the refusal of the Masai warriors to join the King's African Rifles, the British marched upon the Native villages; how, inadvertently, a Masai woman was killed, and how two Hindu shopkeepers were murdered in reprisal by the Murani. And thus, why it was that the thin, red line of Empire had grown slightly redder.

He would tell me old legends sometimes about Mount Kenya, or about the Menegai Crater, called the Mountain of God, or about Kilimanjaro. He would tell me these things and I would ride alongside and ask endless questions, or we would sit together in the jolting buggy and just think about what he had said.

One day, when we were riding to Elkington's, my father spoke about lions.

"Lions are more intelligent than some men," he said, "and more courageous than most. A lion will fight for what he has and for what he needs; he is contemptuous of cowards and wary of his equals. But he is not afraid. You can always trust a lion to be exactly what it is – and never anything else.

"Except," he added, looking more paternally concerned than usual, "that damned lion of Elkington's!"

The Elkington lion was famous within a radius of twelve miles in all directions from the farm, because, if you happened to be anywhere inside that circle, you could hear him roar when he was hungry, when he was sad, or when he just felt like roaring. If, in the night, you lay sleepless on your bed and listened to an intermittent sound that began like the bellow of a banshee trapped in the bowels of Kilimanjaro and ended like the sound of that same banshee suddenly at large and arrived at the foot of your bed, you knew (because you had been told) that this was the song of Paddy.

Two or three of the settlers in East Africa at that time had caught lion cubs and raised them in cages. But Paddy, the Elkington lion, had never seen a cage.

He had grown to full size, tawny, black-maned and muscular, without a worry or a care. He lived on fresh meat, not of his own killing. He spent his waking hours (which coincided with everybody else's sleeping hours) wandering through Elkington's fields and pastures like an affable, if apostrophic, emperor, a-stroll in the gardens of his court.

He thrived on solitude. He had no mate, but pretended indifference and walked alone, not toying too much with imaginings of the unattainable. There were no physical barriers to his freedom, but the lions of the plains do not accept into their respected fraternity an individual bearing in his coat the smell of men. So Paddy ate, slept and roared, and perhaps he sometimes dreamed, but he never left Elkington's. He was a tame lion, Paddy was. He was deaf to the call of the wild.

"I'm always careful of that lion," I told my father, "but he's really harmless. I have seen Mrs Elkington stroke him."

"Which proves nothing," said my father. "A domesticated lion is only an unnatural lion – and whatever is unnatural is untrustworthy."

Whenever my father made an observation as deeply philosophical as that one, and as inclusive, I knew there was nothing more to be said.

I nudged my horse and we broke into a canter covering the remaining distance to Elkington's.

It wasn't a big farm as farms went in Africa before the First World War, but it had a very nice house with a large veranda on which my father, Jim Elkington, Mrs Elkington, and one or two other settlers sat and talked with what to my mind was always unreasonable solemnity.

There were drinks, but beyond that there was a tea-table lavishly spread, as only the English can spread them. I have sometimes thought since of the Elkingtons' tea-table – round, capacious, and white, standing with sturdy legs against the green vines of the garden, a thousand miles of Africa receding from its edge.

It was a mark of sanity, I suppose, less than of luxury. It was evidence of the double debt England still owes to ancient China for her two gifts that made expansion possible – tea and gunpowder.

But cakes and muffins were no fit bribery for me. I had pleasures of my own then, or constant expectations. I made what niggardly salutations I could bring forth from a disinterested memory and left the house at a gait rather faster than a trot.

As I scampered past the square hay shed a hundred yards or so behind the Elkington house, I caught sight of Bishon Singh, whom my father had sent ahead to tend our horses.

I think the Sikh must have been less than forty years old then, but his face was never any indication of his age. On some days he looked thirty and on others he looked fifty, depending on the weather, the time of day, his mood, or the tilt of his turban. If he had ever disengaged his beard from his hair and shaved the one and clipped the other, he might have astonished us all by looking like one of Kipling's elephant boys, but he never did either, and so, to me at least, he remained a man of mystery, without age, or youth, but burdened with experience, like the wandering Jew.

He raised his arm and greeted me in Swahili as I ran through the Elkington farmyard and out towards the open country.

Why I ran at all or with what purpose is beyond my

answering, but when I had no specific destination I always ran as fast as I could in the hope of finding one – and I always found it.

I was within twenty yards of the Elkington lion before I saw him. He lay sprawled in the morning sun, huge, black-maned, and gleaming with life. His tail moved slowly, stroking the rough grass like a knotted rope end. His body was sleek and easy, making a mould where he lay, a cool mould, that would be there when he had gone. He was not asleep; he was only idle. He was rusty-red, and soft, like a strokable cat. I stopped and he lifted his head with magnificent ease and stared at me out of yellow eyes.

I stood there staring back, scuffling my bare toes in the dust, pursing my lips to make a noiseless whistle – a very small girl who knew nothing about lions.

Paddy raised himself then, emitting a little sigh, and began to contemplate me with a kind of quiet premeditation, like that of a slow-witted man fondling an unaccustomed thought.

I cannot say that there was any menace in his eyes, because there wasn't, or that his "frightful jowls" were drooling, because they were handsome jowls and very tidy. He did sniff the air, though, with what impressed me as being close to audible satisfaction. And he did not lie down again.

I remembered the rules that one remembers. I did not run. I walked very slowly, and I began to sing a defiant song.

"Kali coma Simba sisi," I sang. *"Askari yoti ni udari!* – Fierce like the lion are we, Askari all are brave!"

I went in a straight line past Paddy when I sang it, seeing his eyes shine in the thick grass, watching his tail beat time to the metre of my ditty.

"Twendi, twendi – ku pigana – pigna aduoi – piga sana! –

Let us go, let us go – to fight – beat down the enemy! Beat hard, beat hard!"

What lion would not be impressed with the marching song of the King's African Rifles?

Singing it still, I took up my trot toward the rim of the low hill which might, if I were lucky, have Cape gooseberry bushes in its slopes.

The country was grey-green and dry, and the sun lay on it closely, making the ground hot under my bare feet. There was no sound and no wind.

Even Paddy made no sound, coming swiftly behind me.

What I remember most clearly of the moment that followed are three things – a scream that was barely a whisper, a blow that struck me to the ground, and, as I buried my face in my arms and felt Paddy's teeth close on the flesh of my leg, a fantastically bobbing turban, that was Bishon Singh's turban, appear over the edge of the hill.

I remained conscious, but I closed my eyes and tried not to be. It was not so much the pain as it was the sound.

The sound of Paddy's roar in my ears will only be duplicated, I think, when the doors of hell slip their wobbly hinges, one day, and give voice and authenticity to the whole panorama of Dante's poetic nightmares. It was an immense roar that encompassed the world and dissolved me in it.

I shut my eyes very tight, and lay still under the weight of Paddy's paws.

Bishon Singh said afterward that he did nothing. He said he had remained by the hay shed for a few minutes after I ran past him, and then, for no explainable reason had begun to follow me. He admitted, though, that a little while before, he had seen Paddy go in the direction I had taken.

The Sikh called for help, of course, when he saw the lion

meant to attack, and a half-dozen of Elkington's syces had come running from the house. Along with them had come Jim Elkington with a rawhide whip.

Jim Elkington, even without a rawhide whip, was very impressive. He was one of those enormous men whose girths alone seem to preclude any possibility of normal movement, much less of speed. But Jim had speed – not to be loosely compared with lightning, but rather like the speed of something spherical and smooth and relatively irresistible, like the cannonballs of the Napoleonic Wars. Jim was, without question, a man of considerable courage, but in the case of my Rescue From the Lion, it was, I am told, his momentum rather than his bravery for which I must forever be grateful.

It happened like this – as Bishon Singh told it:

"I am resting against the walls of the place where hay is kept and first the large lion and then you, Beru, pass me going toward the open field, and a thought comes to me that a lion and a young girl are strange company, so I follow. I follow to the place where the hill that goes up becomes the hill that goes down, and where it goes down deepest I see that you are running without much thought in your head, and the lion is running behind you with many thoughts in his head, and I scream for everybody to come very fast.

"Everybody comes very fast, but the large lion is faster than anybody, and he jumps on your back and I see you scream but I hear no scream. I only hear the lion, and I begin to run with everybody and this included Bwana Elkington, who is saying a great many words I do not know and is carrying a long kiboko which he is holding in his hand and is meant for beating the large lion.

"Bwana Elkington goes past me the way a man with lighter legs and fewer inches around his stomach might go past me, and he is waving the long kiboko so that it whistles over all our heads like a very sharp wind, but when we get close to the lion it comes to my mind that the lion is not of the mood to accept a kiboko.

"He is standing with the front of himself on your back, Beru, and you are bleeding in three or five places, and he is roaring. I do not believe Bwana Elkington could have thought that that lion at that moment would consent to being beaten, because the lion was not looking the way he had ever looked before when it was necessary for him to be beaten. He was looking as if he did not wish to be disturbed by a kiboko, or the Bwana, or the syces, or Bishon Singh, and he was saying so in a very large voice.

"I believe that Bwana Elkington understood this voice when he was still more than several feet from the lion, and I believe the Bwana considered in his mind that it would be the best thing not to beat the lion just then, but the Bwana when he runs very fast is like the trunk of a great baobab tree rolling down a slope, and it seems that because of this it was not possible for him to explain the thought of his mind to the soles of his feet in a sufficient quickness of time to prevent him from rushing much closer to the lion than in his heart he wished to be.

"And it was in this circumstance, as I am telling it," said Bishon Singh, "which in my considered opinion made it possible for you to be alive, Beru."

"Bwana Elkington rushed at the lion then, Bishon Singh?"

"The lion, as of the contrary, rushed at Bwana Elkington," said Bishon Singh. "The lion deserted you for the Bwana, Beru. The lion was of the opinion that his master was not in any way deserving of a portion of what he, the lion, had accomplished in the matter of fresh meat through no effort by anybody except himself."

Bishon Singh offered this extremely reasonable interpretation with impressive gravity, as if he were expounding the Case For the Lion to a chosen jury of Paddy's peers.

"Fresh meat . . ." I repeated dreamily, and crossed my fingers.

"So then what happened . . .?"

The Sikh lifted his shoulders and let them drop again. "What could happen, Beru? The lion rushed for Bwana Elkington, who in his turn rushed from the lion, and in so rushing did not keep in his hand the long kiboko, but allowed it to fall upon the ground, and in accomplishing this the Bwana was free to ascend a very fortunate tree, which he did."

"And you picked me up, Bishon Singh?"

He made a little dip with his massive turban. "I was happy with the duty of carrying you back to this very bed, Beru, and of advising your father, who had gone to observe some of Bwana Elkington's horses, that you had been moderately eaten by the large lion. Your father returned very fast, and Bwana Elkington some time later returned very fast, but the large lion has not returned at all."

The large lion had not returned at all. That night he killed a horse, and the next night he killed a yearling bullock, and after that a cow fresh for milking.

In the end he was caught and finally caged, but brought to no rendezvous with the firing squad at sunrise. He remained for years in his cage, which, had he managed to live in freedom with his inhibitions, he might never have seen at all.

It seems characteristic of the mind of man that the representation of what is natural to humans must be abhorred, but that what is natural to an infinitely more natural animal must be confined within the bounds of a reason peculiar only to men – more peculiar sometimes than seems reasonable at all.

Paddy lived, people stared at him and he stared back, and this went on until he was an old, old lion. Jim Elkington died, and Mrs Elkington, who really loved Paddy, was forced, because of circumstances beyond her control or Paddy's, to have him shot by Boy Long, the manager of Lord Delamere's estates.

This choice of executioners was, in itself, a tribute to Paddy, for no one loved animals more or understood them better, or could shoot more cleanly than Boy Long.

But the result was the same to Paddy. He had lived and died in ways not of his choosing. He was a good lion. He had done what he could about being a tame lion. Who thinks it just to be judged by a single error?

I still have the scars of his teeth and claws, but they are very small now and almost forgotten, and I cannot begrudge him his moment.

THE CALL OF THE WILD

JACK LONDON

Set in the late 1890s, The Call of the Wild *is the story of Buck, a St Bernard-collie cross-breed. As a young dog he is captured by dog thieves who eventually sell him to be a sled-dog in Alaska during the Klondike gold rush. Only when he meets his new master, Thornton, does he begin to experience any kind of human affection. The bond between man and dog becomes one of absolute trust and respect.*

THAT WINTER, at Dawson, Buck performed another exploit, not so heroic, perhaps, but one that put his name many notches higher on the totem-pole of Alaskan fame. This exploit was particularly gratifying to the three men; for they stood in need of the outfit which it furnished, and were enabled to make a long-desired trip into the virgin East, where miners had not yet appeared. It was brought about by a conversation in the Eldorado Saloon, in which men waxed boastful of their favourite Dogs. Buck, because of his record, was the target for these men, and Thornton was driven stoutly to defend him. At the end of half an hour one man stated that his Dog could start a sled with five hundred pounds and walk off with it;

a second bragged six hundred for his Dog; and a third, seven hundred.

"Pooh! pooh!" said John Thornton; "Buck can start a thousand pounds."

"And break it out? and walk off with it for a hundred yards?" demanded Matthewson, a Bonanza King, he of the seven hundred vaunt.

"And break it out, and walk off with it for a hundred yards," John Thornton said coolly.

"Well," Matthewson said, slowly and deliberately, so that all could hear, "I've got a thousand dollars that says he can't. And there it is." So saying, he slammed a sack of gold dust of the size of a bologna sausage down upon the bar.

Nobody spoke. Thornton's bluff, if bluff it was, had been called. He could feel a flush of warm blood creeping up his face. His tongue had tricked him. He did not know whether Buck could start a thousand pounds. Half a ton! The enormousness of it appalled him. He had great faith in Buck's strength, and had often thought him capable of starting such a load; but never, as now, had he faced the possibility of it, the eyes of a dozen men fixed upon him, silent and waiting. Further, he had no thousand dollars; nor had Hans or Pete.

"I've got a sled standing outside now, with twenty fifty-pound sacks of flour on it," Matthewson went on with brutal directness; "so don't let that hinder you."

Thornton did not reply. He did not know what to say. He glanced from face to face in the absent way of a man who has lost the power of thought and is seeking somewhere to find the thing that will start it going again. The face of Jim O'Brien, a Mastodon King and old-time comrade, caught his eyes. It was as a cue to him, seeming to rouse him to do what he would never have dreamed of doing.

"Can you lend me a thousand?" he asked, almost in a whisper.

"Sure," answered O'Brien, thumping down a plethoric sack by the side of Matthewson's. "Though it's little faith I'm having, John, that the beast can do the trick."

The Eldorado emptied its occupants into the street to see the test. The tables were deserted, and the dealers and gamekeepers came forth to see the outcome of the wager and to lay odds. Several hundred men, furred and mittened, banked around the sled within easy distance. Matthewson's sled, loaded with a thousand pounds of flour, had been standing for a couple of hours, and in the intense cold (it was sixty below zero) the runners had frozen fast to the hard-packed snow. Men offered odds of two to one that Buck could not budge the sled. A quibble arose concerning the phrase "break out". O'Brien contended it was Thornton's privilege to knock the runners loose, leaving Buck to "break it out" from a dead standstill. Matthewson insisted that the phrase included breaking the runners from the frozen grip of the snow. A majority of the men who had witnessed the making of the bet decided in his favour, whereat the odds went up to three to one against Buck.

There were no takers. Not a man believed him capable of the feat. Thornton had been hurried into the wager, heavy with doubt; and now that he looked at the sled itself, the concrete fact, with the regular team of ten Dogs curled up in the snow before it, the more impossible the task appeared. Matthewson waxed jubilant.

"Three to one!" he proclaimed. "I'll lay you another thousand at that figure, Thornton. What d'ye say?"

Thornton's doubt was strong on his face, but his fighting spirit was aroused – the fighting spirit that soars above odds, fails to recognize the impossible, and is deaf to all save the clamour for battle. He called Hans and Pete to him. Their sacks were slim, and with his own the three partners could rake together only two hundred dollars. In the ebb of their fortunes, this sum was their total capital; yet they laid it unhesitatingly against Matthewson's six hundred.

The team of ten Dogs was unhitched; and Buck, with his own harness, was put into the sled. He had caught the contagion of the excitement, and he felt that in some way he must do a great thing for John Thornton. Murmurs of admiration at his splendid appearance went up. He was in perfect condition, without an ounce of superfluous flesh, and the one hundred and fifty pounds that he weighed were so many pounds of grit and virility. His furry coat shone with the sheen of silk. Down the neck and across the shoulders, his mane, in repose as it was, half bristled and seemed to lift with every movement, as though excess of vigour made each particular hair alive and active. The great breast and heavy forelegs were no more than in proportion with the rest of the body, where the muscles showed in tight rolls underneath the skin. Men felt these muscles and proclaimed them hard as iron, and the odds went down to two to one.

"Gad, sir! Gad, sir!" stuttered a member of the latest dynasty, a king of the Skookum Benches. "I offer you eight hundred for him, sir, before the test, sir; eight hundred just as he stands."

Thornton shook his head and stepped to Buck's side

"You must stand off from him," Matthewson protested. "Free play and plenty of room."

The crowd fell silent; only could be heard the voices of the gamblers vainly offering two to one. Everybody acknowledged Buck a magnificent animal, but twenty fifty-pound sacks of flour bulked too large in their eyes for them to loosen their pouch-strings.

Thornton knelt down by Buck's side. He took his head in his two hands and rested cheek on cheek. He did not playfully shake him, as was his wont, or murmur soft love curses; but he whispered in his ear. "As you love me, Buck. As you love me," was what he whispered. Buck whined with suppressed eagerness.

The crowd was watching curiously. The affair was growing mysterious. It seemed like a conjuration. As Thornton got to his feet, Buck seized his mittened hand between his jaws, pressing in with his teeth and releasing loosely, half-reluctantly. It was the answer, in terms, not of speech, but of love. Thornton stepped well back.

"Now, Buck," he said.

Buck tightened the traces, then slacked them for a matter of several inches. It was the way he had learned.

"Gee!" Thornton's voice rang out, sharp in the tense silence.

Buck swung to the right, ending the movement in a plunge that took up the slack and with a sudden jerk arrested his one hundred and fifty pounds. The load quivered, and from under the runners arose a crisp crackling.

"Haw!" Thornton commanded.

Buck duplicated the manoeuvre, this time to the left. The crackling turned into a snapping, the sled pivoting and the runners slipping and grating several inches to the side. The sled was broken out. Men were holding their breaths, intensely unconscious of the fact.

"Now, MUSH!"

Thornton's command cracked out like a pistol shot. Buck threw himself forward, tightening the traces with a jarring lunge. His whole body was gathered compactly together in

the tremendous effort, the muscles writhing and knotting like live things under the silky fur. His great chest was low to the ground, his head forward and down, while his feet were flying like mad, the claws scarring the hard-packed snow in parallel grooves. The sled swayed and trembled, half-started forward. One of his feet slipped, and one man groaned aloud. Then the sled lurched ahead in what appeared a rapid succession of jerks, though it never really came to a dead stop again . . . half an inch . . . an inch . . . two inches . . . The jerks perceptibly diminished; as the sled gained momentum, he caught them up, till it was moving steadily along.

Men gasped and began to breathe again, unaware that for a moment they had ceased to breathe. Thornton was running behind, encouraging Buck with short, cheery words. The distance measured off, and as he neared the pile of firewood which marked the end of the hundred yards, a cheer began to grow and grow, which burst into a roar as he passed the firewood and halted at command. Every man was tearing himself loose, even Matthewson. Hats and mittens were flying in the air. Men were shaking hands, it did not matter with whom, and bubbling over in a general incoherent babel.

But Thornton fell on his knees beside Buck. Head was against head, and he was shaking him back and forth. Those who hurried up heard him cursing Buck, and he cursed him long and fervently, and softly and lovingly.

"Gad, sir! Gad, sir!" spluttered the Skookum Bench king. "I'll give you a thousand for him, sir, a thousand, sir – twelve hundred, sir."

Thornton rose to his feet. His eyes were wet. The tears were streaming frankly down his cheeks. "Sir," he said to the Skookum Bench king, "no, sir. You can go to hell, sir. It's the best I can do for you, sir."

Buck seized Thornton's hand in his teeth. Thornton shook him back and forth. As though animated by a common impulse, the onlookers drew back to a respectful distance; nor were they again indiscreet enough to interrupt.

THE RED PONY

JOHN STEINBECK

The relationship beween man and horse has often been explored in story form – I did it myself in my book War Horse. *But no one has done it better than Steinbeck in his great masterpiece,* The Red Pony, *when he writes of Jody's first meeting with his beloved pony.*

IT WAS FOUR O'CLOCK in the afternoon when Jody topped the hill and looked down on the ranch again. He looked for the saddle horses, but the corral was empty. His father was not back yet. He went slowly, then, toward the afternoon chores. At the ranch house, he found his mother sitting on the porch, mending socks.

"There's two doughnuts in the kitchen for you," she said. Jody slid to the kitchen, and returned with half of one of the doughnuts already eaten and his mouth full. His mother asked him what he had learned in school that day, but she didn't listen to his doughnut-muffled answer. She interrupted: "Jody, tonight see you fill the wood-box clear full. Last night you crossed the sticks and it wasn't only about half full. Lay the sticks flat tonight. And Jody, some of the hens are hiding eggs, or else the dogs are eating them.

Look about in the grass and see if you can find any nests."

Jody, still eating, went out and did his chores. He saw the quail come down to eat with the chickens when he threw out the grain. For some reason his father was proud to have them come. He never allowed any shooting near the house for fear the quail might go away.

When the wood-box was full, Jody took his twenty-two rifle up to the cold spring at the brush line. He drank again and then aimed the gun at all manner of things, at rocks, at birds on the wing, at the big black pig kettle under the cypress tree, but he didn't shoot for he had no cartridges and wouldn't have until he was twelve. If his father had seen him aim the rifle in the direction of the house he would have put the cartridges off another year. Jody remembered this and did not point the rifle down the hill again. Two years was enough to wait for cartridges. Nearly all of his father's presents were given with reservations which hampered their value somewhat. It was good discipline.

The supper waited until dark for his father to return. When at last he came in with Billy Buck, Jody could smell the delicious brandy on their breaths. Inwardly he rejoiced, for his father sometimes talked to him when he smelled of brandy, sometimes even told things he had done in the wild days when he was a boy.

After supper, Jody sat by the fireplace and his shy polite eyes sought the room corners, and he waited for his father to tell what it was he contained, for Jody knew he had news of some sort. But he was disappointed. His father pointed a stern finger at him.

"You'd better go to bed, Jody. I'm going to need you in the morning."

That wasn't so bad. Jody liked to do the things he had to do as long as they weren't routine things. He looked at the floor and his mouth worked out a question before he spoke it. "What are we going to do in the morning, kill a pig?" he asked softly.

"Never you mind. You better get to bed."

When the door was closed behind him, Jody heard his father and Billy Buck chuckling and he knew it was a joke of some kind. And later, when he lay in bed, trying to make words out of the murmurs in the other room, he heard his father protest, "But, Ruth, I didn't give much for him."

Jody heard the hoot-owls hunting the mice down by the barn, and he heard a fruit-tree limb tap-tapping against the house. A cow was lowing when he went to sleep.

When the triangle sounded in the morning, Jody dressed more quickly even than usual. In the kitchen, while he washed his face and combed back his hair, his mother addressed him irritably. "Don't you go out until you get a good breakfast in you."

He went to the dining-room and sat at the long white table. He took a steaming hotcake from the platter, arranged two fried eggs on it, covered them with another hotcake and squashed the whole thing with his fork.

His father and Billy Buck came in. Jody knew from the sound on the floor that both of them were wearing flat-heeled shoes, but he peered under the table to make sure. His father turned off the oil lamp, for the day had arrived, and he looked stern and disciplinary, but Billy Buck didn't look at Jody at all. He avoided the shy questioning eyes of the boy and soaked a whole piece of toast in his coffee.

Carl Tiflin said crossly, "You come with us after breakfast!"

Jody had trouble with his food then, for he felt a kind of doom in the air. After Billy had tilted his saucer and drained the coffee which had slopped into it, and had wiped his hands on his jeans, the two men stood up from the table and went out into the morning light together, and Jody respectfully followed a little behind them. He tried to keep his mind from running ahead, tried to keep it absolutely motionless.

His mother called, "Carl! Don't you let it keep him from school."

They marched past the cypress, where a singletree hung from a limb to butcher the pigs on, and past the black iron kettle, so it was not a pig killing. The sun shone over the hill and threw long, dark shadows of the trees and buildings. They crossed a stubble-field to shortcut to the barn. Jody's father unhooked the door and they went in. They had been walking toward the sun on the way down. The barn was black as night in contrast and warm from the hay and from the beasts. Jody's father moved over towards the one box stall. "Come here!" he ordered. Jody could begin to see things now. He looked into the box stall and then stepped back quickly.

A red pony colt was looking at him out of the stall. Its tense ears were forward and a light of disobedience was in its eyes. Its coat was rough and thick as an airedale's fur and its mane was long and tangled. Jody's throat collapsed in on itself and cut his breath short.

"He needs a good currying," his father said, "and if I ever hear of you not feeding him or leaving his stall dirty, I'll sell him off in a minute."

Jody couldn't bear to look at the pony's eyes any more. He gazed down at his hands for a moment, and he asked very shyly, "Mine?" No one answered him. He put his hand out towards the pony. Its grey nose came close, sniffing loudly, and then the lips drew back and the strong teeth closed on Jody's fingers. The pony shook its head up and down and seemed to laugh with amusement. Jody regarded his bruised fingers. "Well," he said with pride – "well, I guess he can bite all right." The two men laughed, somewhat in relief. Carl Tiflin went out of the barn and walked up a side-hill to be by himself, for he was embarrassed, but Billy Buck stayed. It was easier to talk to Billy Buck. Jody asked again – "Mine?"

Billy became professional in tone. "Sure! That is, if you look out for him and break him right. I'll show you how. He's just a colt. You can't ride him for some time."

Jody put out his bruised hand again, and this time the red pony let his nose be rubbed. "I ought to have a carrot," Jody said. "Where'd we get him, Billy?"

"Bought him at a sheriff's auction," Billy explained. "A show went broke in Salinas and had debts. The sheriff was selling off their stuff."

The pony stretched out his nose and shook the forelock from his wild eyes. Jody stroked the nose a little. He said softly, "There isn't a – saddle?"

Billy Buck laughed. "I'd forgot. Come along."

In the harness-room he lifted down a little saddle of red morocco leather. "It's just a show saddle," Billy Buck said disparagingly. "It isn't practical for the brush, but it was cheap at the sale."

Jody couldn't trust himself to look at the saddle either, and he couldn't speak at all. He brushed the shining red leather with his fingertips, and after a long time he said, "It'll look pretty on him though." He thought of the grandest and prettiest things he knew. "If he hasn't a name already, I think I'll call him Gabilan Mountains," he said.

Billy Buck knew how he felt. "It's a pretty long name. Why don't you just call him Gabilan? That means hawk. That would be a fine name for him." Billy felt glad. "If you will collect tail hair, I might be able to make a hair rope for you sometime. You could use it for a hackamore."

Jody wanted to go back to the box stall. "Could I lead him to school, do you think – to show the kids?"

But Billy shook his head. "He's not even halter-broke yet. We had a time getting him here. Had to almost drag him. You better be starting for school though."

"I'll bring the kids to see him here this afternoon," Jody said.

Six boys came over the hill half an hour early that afternoon, running hard, their heads down, their forearms working, their breath whistling. They swept by the house and cut across the stubble-field to the barn. And then they stood self-consciously before the pony, and then they looked at Jody with eyes in which there was a new admiration and a new respect. Before today Jody had been a boy, dressed in overalls and a blue shirt – quieter than most, even suspected of being a little cowardly. And now he was different. Out of a thousand centuries they drew the ancient admiration of the footman for the horseman. They knew instinctively that a man on a horse is spiritually as well as physically bigger than a man on foot. They knew that Jody had been miraculously lifted out of equality with them, and had been placed over them. Gabilan put his head out of the stall and sniffed them.

"Why'n't you ride him?" the boys cried. "Why'n't you braid his tail with ribbons like in the fair?" "When you going to ride him?"

Jody's courage was up. He too felt the superiority of the horseman. "He's not old enough. Nobody can ride him for a long time. I'm going to train him on the long halter. Billy Buck is going to show me how."

"Well, can't we even lead him around a little?"

"He isn't even halter-broke," Jody said. He wanted to be

completely alone when he took the pony out for the first time. "Come and see the saddle."

They were speechless at the red morocco saddle, completely shocked out of comment. "It isn't much use in the brush," Jody explained. "It'll look pretty on him though. Maybe I'll ride bareback when I go into the brush."

"How you going to rope a cow without a saddle horn?"

"Maybe I'll get another saddle for everyday. My father might want me to help him with the stock." He let them feel the red saddle, and showed them the brass chain throat-latch on the bridle and the big brass buttons at each temple where the headstall and brow band crossed. The whole thing was too wonderful. They had to go away after a little while, and each boy, in his mind, searched among his possessions for a bribe worthy of offering in return for a ride on the red pony when the time should come.

Jody was glad when they had gone. He took brush and currycomb from the wall, took down the barrier of the box stall and stepped cautiously in. The pony's eyes glittered, and he edged around into kicking position. But Jody touched him on the shoulder and rubbed his high arched neck as he had always seen Billy Buck do, and he crooned, "So-o-o, boy," in a deep voice. The pony gradually relaxed his tenseness. Jody curried and brushed until a pile of dead hair lay in the stall and until the pony's coat had taken on a deep red shine. Each time he finished he thought it might have been done better. He braided the mane into a dozen little pigtails, and he braided the forelock, and then he undid them and brushed the hair out straight again.

Jody did not hear his mother enter the barn. She was angry when she came, but when she looked in at the pony and at Jody working over him, she felt a curious pride rise up in her. "Have you forgot the wood-box?" she asked gently. "It's not far off from dark and there's not a stick of wood in the house, and the chickens aren't fed."

Jody quickly put up his tools. "I forgot, ma'am."

"Well, after this do your chores first. Then you won't forget. I expect you'll forget lots of things now if I don't keep an eye on you."

"Can I have carrots from the garden for him, ma'am?"

She had to think about that. "Oh – I guess so, if you only take the big tough ones."

"Carrots keep the coat good," he said, and again she felt the curious rush of pride.

Jody never waited for the triangle to get him out of bed after the coming of the pony. It became his habit to creep out of bed even before his mother was awake, to slip into his clothes and to go quietly down to the barn to see Gabilan. In the grey quiet mornings when the land and the brush and the houses and the trees were silver-grey and black like a photograph negative, he stole towards the barn, past the sleeping stones and the sleeping cypress tree. The turkeys, roosting in the tree out of coyotes' reach, clicked drowsily. The fields glowed with a grey frost-like light and in the dew the tracks of rabbits and of fieldmice stood out sharply. The good dogs came stiffly out of their little houses, hackles up and deep growls in their throats. Then they caught Jody's scent, and their stiff tails rose up and waved a greeting – Doubletree Mutt with the big thick tail, and Smasher, the incipient shepherd – then went lazily back to their warm beds.

It was a strange time and a mysterious journey, to Jody – an extension of a dream. When he first had the pony he liked to torture himself during the trip by thinking Gabilan would not be in his stall, and worse, would never have been there. And he had other delicious little self-induced pains. He thought how the rats had gnawed ragged holes in the red saddle, and how the mice had nibbled Gabilan's tail until it was stringy and thin. He usually ran the last little way to the barn. He unlatched the rusty hasp of the barn door and stepped in, and no matter how quietly he opened the door, Gabilan was always looking at him over the barrier of the box stall and Gabilan whinnied softly and stamped his front foot, and his eyes had big sparks of red fire in them like oakwood embers.

Sometimes, if the work-horses were to be used that day, Jody found Billy Buck in the barn harnessing and currying. Billy stood with him and looked long at Gabilan and he told Jody a great many things about horses. He explained that they were terribly afraid for their feet, so that one must make a practice of lifting the legs and patting the hooves and ankles to remove their terror. He told Jody how horses love conversation. He must talk to the pony all the time, and tell him the reasons for everything. Billy wasn't sure a horse could understand everything that was said to him, but it was impossible to say how much was understood. A horse never kicked up a fuss if someone he liked explained things to him. Billy could give examples, too. He had known, for instance, a horse nearly deadbeat with fatigue to perk up when told it was only a little farther to his destination. And he had known a horse paralysed with fright to come out of it when his rider told him what it was that was frightening him. While he talked in the mornings, Billy Buck cut twenty or thirty straws into neat three-inch lengths and stuck them into his hatband. Then, during the whole day, if he wanted to pick his teeth or merely to chew on something, he had only to reach up for one of them.

Jody listened carefully, for he knew and the whole country knew that Billy Buck was a fine hand with horses. Billy's own horse was a stringy cayuse with a hammer head, but he nearly always won the first prizes at the stock trials. Billy could rope a steer, take a double half-hitch about the horn with his riata, and dismount, and his horse would play the steer as an angler plays a fish, keeping a tight rope until the steer was down or beaten.

Every morning, after Jody had curried and brushed the pony, he let down the barrier of the stall, and Gabilan thrust past him and raced down the barn and into the corral. Around and around he galloped, and sometimes he jumped forward and landed on stiff legs. He stood quivering, stiff ears forward, eyes rolling so that the whites showed, pretending to be frightened. At last he walked snorting to the water-trough and buried his nose in the water up to the nostrils. Jody was proud then, for he knew that was the way to judge a horse. Poor horses only touched their lips to the water, but a fine spirited beast put his whole nose and mouth under, and only left room to breathe.

Then Jody stood and watched the pony, and he saw things he had never noticed about any other horse, the sleek, sliding flank muscles and the cords of the buttocks, which flexed like a closing fist, and the shine the sun put on the red coat. Having seen horses all his life, Jody had never looked at them very closely before. But now he noticed the moving ears which gave expression and even inflection of expression to the face. The pony talked with his ears. You could tell exactly how he felt about everything by the way his ears pointed. Sometimes they were stiff and upright and sometimes lax and sagging. They went back when he was angry or fearful, and forward when he was anxious and curious and pleased; and their exact position indicated which emotion he had.

Billy Buck kept his word. In the early fall the training began. First there was the halter-breaking, and that was the

hardest because it was the first thing. Jody held a carrot and coaxed and promised and pulled on the rope. The pony set his feet like a burro when he felt the strain. But before long he learned. Jody walked all over the ranch leading him. Gradually he took to dropping the rope until the pony followed him unled wherever he went.

And then came the training on the long halter. That was slower work. Jody stood in the middle of a circle, holding the long halter. He clucked with his tongue and the pony started to walk in a big circle, held in by the long rope. He clucked again to make the pony trot, and again to make him gallop. Around and around Gabilan went thundering and enjoying it immensely. Then he called, "Whoa," and the pony stopped. It was not long until Gabilan was perfect at it. But in many ways he was a bad pony. He bit Jody in the pants and stomped on Jody's feet. Now and then his ears went back and he aimed a tremendous kick at the boy. Every time he did one of these bad things, Gabilan settled back and seemed to laugh to himself.

Billy Buck worked at the hair rope in the evenings before the fireplace. Jody collected tail hair in a bag, and he sat and watched Billy slowly constructing the rope, twisting a few hairs to make a string and rolling two strings together for a cord, and then braiding a number of cords to make the rope. Billy rolled the finished rope on the floor under his foot to make it round and hard.

The long halter work rapidly approached perfection. Jody's father, watching the pony stop and start and trot and gallop, was a little bothered by it.

"He's getting to be almost a trick pony," he complained. "I don't like trick horses. It takes all the – dignity out of a horse to make him do tricks. Why, a trick horse is kind of like an actor – no dignity, no character of his own." And his father said, "I guess you better be getting him used to the saddle pretty soon."

Jody rushed for the harness-room. For some time he had been riding the saddle on a sawhorse. He changed the stirrup length over and over, and could never get it just right. Sometimes, mounted on the sawhorse in the harness-room, with collars and hames and tugs hung all about him, Jody rode out beyond the room. He carried his rifle across the pommel. He saw the fields go flying by, and he heard the beat of the galloping hoofs.

WAITING FOR ANYA

MICHAEL MORPURGO

I stayed for a while in Lescun in France where I set this novel. I walked the Pyrenees, encountered angry sheep dogs, saw my first European bear, watched eagles soaring over the peaks. I discovered the village was occupied by German border guards during the Second World War. Many Jewish people and others escaped over the mountains to neutral Spain. Many French people risked their lives to help them.

In my novel, Jo is drawn into greater and greater danger as he plays his own part in helping dozens of children to safety. It is his terrifying encounter with the bear, in this extract, that begins his story.

JO SHOULD HAVE KNOWN BETTER. After all Papa had told him often enough: "Whittle a stick Jo, pick berries, eat, look for your eagle if you must," he'd said, "but do something. You sit doing nothing on a hillside in the morning sun with the tinkle of sheep bells all about you and you're bound to drop off. You've got to keep your eyes busy, Jo. If your eyes are busy then they won't let your brain go to sleep. And whatever you do, Jo, never lie down. Sit down but don't lie down." Jo knew all that, but he'd been up since half past five that morning and milked a hundred sheep. He was tired, and anyway the sheep seemed settled enough grazing the pasture below him. Rouf lay beside him, his head on his paws, watching the sheep. Only his eyes moved.

Jo lay back on the rock and considered the lark rising above him and wondered why larks seem to perform when the sun shines. He could hear the church bells of Lescun in the distance but only faintly. Lescun, his village, his valley, where the people lived for their sheep and their cows. And they lived with them too. Half of each house was given over to the animals, a dairy on the ground floor, a hay loft above; and in front of every house was a walled yard that served as a permanent sheep fold.

For Jo the village was his whole world. He'd only been out of it a few times in all his twelve years, and one of those was to the railway station just two years before to see his father off to the war. They'd all gone, all the men who weren't too young and who weren't too old. It wouldn't take long to hammer the Boche and they'd be back home again. But when the news had come it had all been bad, so bad you couldn't believe it. There were rumours first of retreat and then of defeat, of French armies disintegrating, of English armies driven into the sea. Jo did not believe any of it at first, nor did anyone; but then one morning outside the Mairie he saw Grandpère crying openly in the street and he had to believe it. Then they heard that Jo's father was a prisoner-of-war in Germany and so were all the others who had gone from the village; except Jean Marty, cousin Jean, who would never be coming back. Jo lay there and tried to picture Jean's face; he could not. He could remember his dry cough though and the way he would spring down a mountain like a deer. Only Hubert could run faster than Jean. Hubert Sarthol was the giant of the village. He had the mind of a child and could only speak a few recognizable words. The rest of his talk was a miscellany of grunting and groaning and squeaking but somehow he managed to make himself more or less understood. Jo remembered how Hubert had cried when they told him he couldn't join the army like the others. The bells of Lescun and the bells of the sheep blended in soporific harmony to lull him away into his dreams.

Rouf was the kind of dog that didn't need to bark too often. He was a massive white mountain dog, old and stiff in his legs but still top dog in the village and he knew it. He was barking now though, a gruff roar of a bark that woke Jo instantly. He sat up. The sheep were gone. Rouf roared again from somewhere behind him, from in among the trees. The sheep bells were loud with alarm, their cries shrill and strident. Jo was on his feet and whistling for Rouf to bring them back. They scattered out of the wood and came running and leaping down towards him. Jo thought it was a lone sheep at first that had got itself caught up on the edge of the wood, but then it barked as it backed away and became Rouf – Rouf rampant, hackles up, snarling; and there was blood on his side. Jo ran towards him calling him back and it was then that he saw the bear and stopped dead. As the bear came out into the sunlight she stood up, her nose lifted in the air. Rouf stayed his ground, his body shaking with fury as he barked.

The nearest Jo had ever been to a bear before was to the bearskin that hung on the wall in the café. Stood up as she was she was as tall as a full-grown man, her coat a creamy brown, her snout black. Jo could not find his voice to shout with, he could not find his legs to run with. He stood mesmerized, quite unable to take his eyes off the bear. A terrified ewe blundered into him and knocked him over. Then he was on his feet, and without even a look over his shoulder he was running down towards the village. He

careered down the slopes, his arms flailing to keep his balance. Several times he tumbled and rolled and picked himself up again, but as he gathered speed his legs would run away with him once more. All it needed was a rock or a tussock of grass to send him sprawling once again. Bruised and bloodied he reached the track to the village and ran, legs pumping, head back, and shouting whenever he could find the breath to do it.

By the time he reached the village – and never had it taken so long – he hadn't the breath to say more than one word, but one word was all he needed. "Bear!" he cried and pointed back to the mountains, but he had to repeat it several times before they seemed to understand or perhaps before they would believe him. Then his mother had him by the shoulders and was trying to make herself heard through the hubbub of the crowd about them.

"Are you all right, Jo? Are you hurt?" she said.

"Rouf, Maman," he gasped. "There's blood all over him."

"The sheep," Grandpère shouted. "What about the sheep?"

Jo shook his head. "I don't know," he said. "I don't know."

Monsieur Sarthol, Hubert's father and mayor of the village as long as Jo had been alive, was trying to organize loudly; but no one was paying him much attention. They had gone for their guns and for their dogs. Within minutes they were all gathered in the Square, some on horseback but most on foot. Those children that could be caught were shut indoors in the safekeeping of grandmothers, mothers or aunts; but many escaped their clutches and dived unseen into the narrow streets to join up with the hunting party as it left the village. A bear hunt was once in a lifetime and not to be missed. This was the stuff of legends and here was one in the making. Jo pleaded with Grandpère to be allowed to go but Grandpère could do nothing for him, Maman would have none of it. He was bleeding profusely from his nose and his knee, so despite all his objections he was bustled away into the house to have his wounds cleaned and bandaged. Christine, his small sister, gazed up at him with big eyes as Maman wiped away the blood.

"Where's the bear, Jo?" Christine asked. "Where's the bear?"

Maman kept saying he was as pale as a ghost and should go and lie down. He appealed one last time to Grandpère, but Grandpère ruffled his hair proudly, took his hunting rifle from the corner of the room and went out with everyone else to hunt the bear.

"Was it big, Jo?" said Christine tugging at his arm. She was full of questions. You could never ignore Christine or her questions – she wouldn't let you. "Was it as big as Hubert?" And she held up her hands as high as she could.

"Bigger," said Jo.

Bandaged like a wounded soldier he was taken up to his bedroom and tucked under the blankets. He stayed in bed only until Maman left the room, and then he sprang out of bed and ran to the window. He could see nothing but the narrow streets and the grey roofs of the village, and beyond the church-tower just a glimpse of the jagged mountain peaks still white in places with winter snow. The streets were empty of people, all except the priest, Father Lasalle, who was hurrying past, his hand on his hat to stop it blowing away.

All afternoon Jo watched as the clouds came down and began to swallow the valley. It was just after the church clock struck five that he heard a distant baying of dogs and shortly after a volley of shots that echoed through the mountains and left a terrible silence hanging over the village.

He was down in the Square half an hour later with everyone else to watch the triumphant procession as it wound its way through the streets. Grandpère came first, Hubert gambolling alongside him.

"We got her," Grandpère was shouting. "We got her. Give us a hand here Hubert, give us a hand." And they disappeared together into the café. They brought out two chairs each and set them down in front of the war memorial.

Limp in death, carried on two long poles by four men, the bear rocked into view, blood on her lolling tongue. She was laid out on the chairs, her legs hanging down on either side, her snout pressed up against the back of a chair. Jo was looking everywhere for Rouf but could not find him. He asked Grandpère if he had seen him but like everyone else Grandpère was too busy telling the story of the hunt or having his photograph taken. It was the grocer, Armand Jollet, who took pride of place in the photograph; it seemed he was the one who had actually shot the bear. He proclaimed this noisily, his round face red with pride and exhilaration. "Two hundred metres away I was, and I hit him right between the eyes."

"It's a she," said Father Lasalle bending over the bear.

"What's the difference?" said Armand Jollet. "He or she, that skin's worth a fortune."

In the celebrations that followed the photograph, the war was suddenly forgotten. Even Marie, Cousin Jean's widow, was laughing with them, swept along on a tide of communal joy and relief. Hubert clapped and cavorted about the place like a wild thing. He reared up like a bear and roared around the streets chasing screaming children and shouting, "Baar! Baar!" Jo looked down at the bear and stroked her back. The fur was long and close and soft, the body still warm with life. Blood from the bear's nose dropped on to his shoe and he felt suddenly sick. He turned to run away but Monsieur Sarthol had his arm around his shoulders and was calling for silence.

"Here's the lad himself," he said. "Without Jo Lalande there'd be no bear. This is the first bear we have shot in Lescun for over twenty-five years."

"Thirty," said Father Lasalle.

The Mayor ignored him and went on. "Lord knows how many of our sheep she'd have killed. We've a lot to thank him for." Jo saw Maman's eyes smiling back at him in the front of the crowd but he could not smile back. The Mayor lifted his glass – most people seemed to have a glass in their hand by now. "So, here's to Jo and here's to the bear, and down with the Boche."

"Long live the bear," someone shouted and the laughter that followed echoed in Jo's head. He could stand it no longer. He pulled away and ran, ignoring Maman's call to come back.

Until the Mayor's speech he had not thought about his part in it all. The she-bear was lying there dead, spread out on the chairs in the Square and he knew now it was all his doing. And perhaps Rouf was out there in the hills with his throat torn out, and none of it would have happened if he had not fallen asleep.

He ran all the way back along the track to the sheep pastures and up towards the trees. He stood there and called Rouf again and again until his voice cracked, but only the crows answered him. He pushed the tears back out of his eyes and tried to calm himself, to remember the exact spot where he'd last seen Rouf. He called again, he whistled; but the clouds seemed to soak up the echoes. He looked up. There were no longer any mountains to be seen above the tree line, only a pall of thick mist. It was still now, not a whisper of wind. He could see where the sheep had been; there was wool caught on the bark of the trees, there were droppings here, footprints there. And then he saw the blood, Rouf's blood perhaps, a brown smattering on the root of a tree.

He could not be sure what it was that he was hearing, not at first. He thought perhaps it was the mewing of an invisible buzzard flying through the clouds but then he heard the sound again and knew it for what it was, the whining of a dog – high-pitched and distant but now quite unmistakable. He called and he climbed, it was too steep to run. He ducked under low-slung branches, he clambered over fallen trees calling all the while: "I'm coming Rouf, I'm coming."

The whining was punctuated now with a strange, intermittent growling, quite unlike anything he had heard before. He came upon Rouf sooner than he had expected. He spotted him through the trees sitting still as a rock, his head lowered as if he was pointing. He did not even turn around to look as Jo broke through into the clearing behind him. He seemed intent upon something in the mouth of a small cave. It was brown and it was small; and then it moved and became a bear cub. It was sitting in the shadows and waving one of its front paws at Rouf. Jo crouched down and put a hand on Rouf's neck. Rouf looked up at him whining with excitement. He licked his lips and resumed his focus on the bear cub, his body taut. The bear cub rocked back against the side of the cave, legs apart, and growled. Yet it was hardly a growl, more a bleat of hunger, a cry for help, a call for mother. "They'll kill him, Rouf," he whispered. "If they find out about him they'll hunt him down and kill him, just like his mother." Still looking at the bear he stroked Rouf's neck. It was matted and wet to the touch – like blood – but when he looked down at Rouf there wasn't a mark on him.

Suddenly Rouf was on his feet, he swung round, hackles up, a rumbling growl in his throat. Jo turned. There was a man standing under the trees at the edge of the clearing. He wore a dirty black coat, a battered hat on his head. They looked at each other. Rouf stopped growling and his tail began to wag.

"Only me again," said the man coming out of the trees towards them. Even with his hat he was a short man and as he came closer Jo saw that he had the gaunt, grey look of old men, yet his beard was rust red with not a fleck of white in it. There was a wine bottle in one hand and a stick in the other.

"Milk," he said holding out the bottle. Rouf sniffed at it and the man laughed. "Not for you," he said and he patted Rouf on the head. "For the little fellow. Starving he is. Perhaps you'd hold my stick for me," he said. "We don't want to frighten him do we?" He gave his hat to Jo as well and took off his coat. "I saw the whole thing, you know. I saw you running off too. Your dog is he?" Jo nodded. "Fights like a tiger doesn't he? Bears like that can knock your head off you know. One swipe of the paw that's all it takes. He was lucky. She tore his ear a bit, a lot of blood; but we soon cleaned you up didn't we old son? Right as rain he is now." He bent down and poured some milk on to a rock. "Now, let's see if we can get this little fellow to take a drink." He backed away a few paces and knelt down. "He'll smell it soon, you'll see. Give him time and he won't be able to resist it." He sat back on his heels.

The cub ventured out of the shadows of the cave, lifting his nose and sniffing the air as he came. "Come on, come on little fellow," said the man, "we won't hurt you." And he reached out very slowly and poured out some more milk but closer to the bear cub this time. "She could've got away you know."

"Who?" said Jo.

"The bear, the mother bear. I've been thinking about it. She was leading them away from her cub. Deliberate it was, I'm sure of it. And what's more she led them a fair old dance I can tell you. Did you see the hunt?" Jo shook his head. "Right away down the valley she took them. I saw it all – well most of it anyway. Course I couldn't know why she was doing that, not at the time; and then I was on my way back home through the woods and there was this little fellow, and your dog just sitting here watching him. Covered in blood he was. Once I'd cleaned him up I went back home for some milk – the only thing I could think of. There you are, he's coming for it now." The cub came forward tentatively, touched the milk with his paw, smelt it, licked it to taste and then began to lap noisily. Suddenly the man's free arm shot out and scooped the cub on to his lap. There was a flurry of paws and a furious scratching and yowling until all the flailing arms and legs were trapped. His whole head was white with milk by now but the end of the bottle was in his mouth and he was sucking in deeply. The man looked up at Jo and smiled. He had milk all over his beard and was licking his lips. "Got him," he said and he chuckled until he laughed. The cub still clung to the bottle when it was empty and would not let go.

"He'll die out here on his own won't he?" said Jo.

"No he won't, not if we don't let him," said the man and he tickled the cub under his chin. "Someone's going to have to look after him."

"I can't," said Jo. "They'd kill him. If I took him home they'd kill him. I know they would." He touched the pad of the cub's paw, it was harder than he'd expected. The man thought for a while nodding slowly.

"Well then, I'll have to do it, won't I?" he said. "Won't be long, only a month or two at the most I should think and then he'll be able to cope on his own. I've got nothing much else to do with myself, not at the moment." For just a moment as he caught his eye Jo thought he recognized the man from somewhere before but he could not think where. Yet he was sure he knew everyone who lived in the valley – not by name necessarily, but by place or by face. "You don't know who I am do you?" said the man. It was as if he could read Jo's thoughts. Jo shook his head. "Well that makes us even doesn't it, because I don't know you either. Maybe it's better it stays that way. You've got to promise me never to say a word, you understand?" There was a new urgency in his voice. "There was no cub, you never met me, you never even saw me. None of this ever happened." He reached out and gripped Jo's arm tightly. "You have to promise me. Not a word to anyone – not your father, not your mother, not your best friend, no one, not ever."

"All right," said Jo who was becoming alarmed. He felt the grip on his arm relax.

"Good boy, good boy," he said and patted Jo's arm.

The man looked up. The mist was filtering down through the treetops above them. "I'd better get back," he said. "I don't want to get caught out in this, I'll never find my way home."

Once he was on his feet Jo gave him his hat and his stick. "Now you hang on to that dog of yours," he said. "I don't want him following me home. Where one goes others can follow, if you understand my meaning." Jo wasn't sure he did. The cub clambered up his shoulder and put an arm around his neck. "Seems to like me, doesn't he?" said the man. He turned to go and then stopped. "And don't you go blaming yourself for what happened this afternoon. You had your job to do, and that old mother bear she had hers to do and that's all there is to it. Besides," and he smiled broadly as the cub snuffled in his ear, "besides, if none of it had happened, we'd never have met would we?"

"We haven't met," said Jo catching Rouf by the scruff of his neck as he made to follow them. The man laughed.

"Nor we have," he said. "Nor we have. And if we haven't met we can't say goodbye can we?" And he turned, waved his stick above his head and walked away into the trees, the cub's chin resting on his shoulder. The eyes that looked back at Jo were two little moons of milk.

ANDROCLES AND THE LION

Retold by ANDREW LANG

Without sentimentality, this story illustrates that there can exist a great bond of trust and understanding between ourselves and our fellow creatures. It may be legend, it may be fact. Either way it is utterly believable – but that may be the way it is told. It is all in the telling.

MANY HUNDRED YEARS AGO, there lived in the north of Africa a poor Roman slave called Androcles. His master held great power and authority in the country, but he was a hard, cruel man, and his slaves led a very unhappy life. They had little to eat, had to work hard, and were often punished and tortured if they failed to satisfy their master's caprices. For long, Androcles had borne with the hardships of his life; but at last he could bear it no longer, and he made up his mind to run away. He knew that it was a great risk, for he had no friends in that foreign country with whom he could seek safety and protection; and he was aware that if he was overtaken and caught, he would be put to a cruel death.

But even death, he thought, would not be so hard as the

life he now led, and it was possible that he might escape to the sea coast, and somehow some day get back to Rome and find a kinder master.

So he waited till the old moon had waned to a tiny gold thread in the skies, and then, one dark night, he slipped out of his master's house, and, creeping through the deserted forum and along the silent town, he passed out of the city into the vineyards and cornfields lying outside the walls. In the cool night air, he walked rapidly. From time to time he was startled by the sudden barking of a Dog, or the sound of voices coming from some late revellers in the villas which stood beside the road along which he hurried. But as he got farther into the country, these sounds ceased, and there was silence and darkness all round him. When the sun rose, he had already gone many miles away from the town in which he had been so miserable.

But now a new terror oppressed him – the terror of great loneliness. He had got into a wild, barren country, where there was no sign of human habitation. A thick growth of low trees and thorny mimosa bushes spread out before him, and as he tried to thread his way through them, he was severely scratched, and his scant garments torn by the long thorns. Besides, the sun was very hot, and the trees were not high enough to afford him any shade. He was worn out with hunger and fatigue, and he longed to lie down and rest. But to lie down in that fierce sun would have meant death; and he struggled on, hoping to find some wild berries to eat, and some water to quench his thirst.

But when he came out of the scrub wood, he found he was as badly off as before. A long, low line of rocky cliffs rose before him, but there were no houses, and he saw no hope of finding food. He was so tired that he could not wander farther; and seeing a cave which looked cool and dark in the side of the cliffs, he crept into it, and, stretching his tired limbs on the sandy floor, fell fast asleep.

Suddenly he was awakened by a noise that made his blood run cold. The roar of a wild beast sounded in his ears, and as he started trembling and in terror to his feet, he beheld a huge, tawny Lion, with great glistening white teeth, standing in the entrance of the cave. It was impossible to fly, for the Lion barred the way. Immovable with fear, Androcles stood rooted to the spot, waiting for the Lion to spring on him and tear him limb from limb.

But the Lion did not move. Making a low moan as if in great pain, it stood licking its huge paw, from which Androcles now saw that blood was flowing freely. Seeing the poor animal in such pain, and noticing how gentle it seemed, Androcles forgot his own terror, and slowly approached the Lion, who held up its paw as if asking the man to help it. Then Androcles saw that a monster thorn had entered the paw, making a deep cut, and causing great pain and swelling. Swiftly but firmly he drew the thorn out, and pressed the swelling to try to stop the flowing of the blood. Relieved of the pain, the Lion quietly lay down at Androcles' feet, slowly moving his great bushy tail from side to side as a Dog does when it feels happy and comfortable.

From that moment, Androcles and the Lion became devoted friends. After lying for a little while at his feet, licking the poor wounded paw, the Lion got up and limped out of the cave. A few moments later, it returned with a little dead Rabbit in its mouth, which it put down on the floor of the cave beside Androcles. The poor man, who was starving with hunger, cooked the Rabbit somehow, and ate it. In the evening, led by the Lion, he found a place where there was a spring, at which he quenched his dreadful thirst.

And so for three years, Androcles and the Lion lived

together in the cave; wandering about the woods together by day, sleeping together at night. For in summer, the cave was cooler than the woods, and in winter it was warmer.

At last, the longing in Androcles' heart to live once more with his fellow men became so great that he felt he could remain in the woods no longer, but that he must return to a town, and take his chance of being caught and killed as a runaway slave. And so, one morning, he left the cave, and wandered away in the direction where he thought the sea and the large towns lay. But in a few days, he was captured by a band of soldiers who were patrolling the country in search of fugitive slaves, and he was put in chains and sent as a prisoner to Rome.

Here he was cast into prison and tried for the crime of having run away from his master. He was condemned as a punishment to be torn to pieces by wild beasts on the first public holiday, in the great circus at Rome.

When the day arrived, Androcles was brought out of his prison, dressed in a simple, short tunic, and with a scarf round his right arm. He was given a lance with which to defend himself – a forlorn hope, as he knew that he had to fight with a powerful Lion which had been kept without food for some days to make it more savage and bloodthirsty. As he stepped into the arena of the huge circus, above the roar of the voices of thousands on thousands of spectators, he could hear the savage roar of the wild beasts from their cages below the floor on which he stood.

Of a sudden, the silence of expectation fell on the spectators, for a signal had been given, and the cage containing the Lion with which Androcles had to fight had been shot up into the arena from the floor below. A great animal had sprung out of its cage into the arena, and with a bound had rushed at the spot where Androcles had stood

trembling. But suddenly, as he saw Androcles, the Lion stood still, wondering. Then quickly but quietly it approached him, and gently moved its tail and licked the man's hands, and fawned upon him like a great Dog. And Androcles patted the Lion's head, and gave a sob of recognition, for he knew that it was his own Lion, with whom he had lived and lodged all those months and years.

And, seeing this strange and wonderful meeting between the man and the wild beast, all the people marvelled; and the emperor, from his high seat above the arena, sent for Androcles, and bade him tell his story and explain this mystery. And the emperor was so delighted with the story that he said Androcles was to be released and to be made a free man from that hour. And he rewarded him with money, and ordered that the Lion was to belong to him, and to accompany him wherever he went.

And when the people in Rome met Androcles walking, followed by his faithful Lion, they used to point at them and say: "That is the Lion, the guest of the man, and that is the man, the doctor of the Lion."

THE TIGER, THE BRAHMAN, AND THE JACKAL

Retold by JOSEPH JACOBS

Many folk tales use animals and their characterization to illustrate human frailties and moral dilemmas. Joseph Jacobs in his retelling of this traditional Indian tale does just this – the storyweaving is deft, and everything is implicit.

ONCE UPON A TIME, a Tiger was caught in a trap. He tried in vain to get out through the bars, and rolled and bit with rage and grief when he failed.

By chance a poor Brahman came by. "Let me out of this cage, oh, pious one!" cried the Tiger.

"Nay, my friend," replied the Brahman mildly; "you would probably eat me if I did."

"Not at all!" swore the Tiger with many oaths; "on the contrary, I should be forever grateful, and serve you as a slave!"

Now, when the Tiger sobbed and sighed and wept and swore, the pious Brahman's heart softened; and at last he consented to open the door of the cage. Out popped the Tiger, and, seizing the poor man, cried, "What a fool you are! What is to prevent my eating you now; for after being cooped up so long, I am just terribly hungry?"

In vain the Brahman pleaded for his life; the most he could gain was a promise to abide by the decision of the first three things he chose to question as to the justice of the Tiger's action.

So the Brahman first asked a pipal tree what it thought of the matter, but the pipal tree relied coldly, "What have you to complain about? Don't I give shade and shelter to everyone who passes by, and don't they in return tear down my branches to feed their Cattle? Don't whimper – be a man!"

Then the Brahman, sad at heart, went farther afield till he saw a Buffalo turning a well-wheel; but he fared no better from it, for it answered: "You are a fool to expect gratitude! Look at me! While I gave milk, they fed me on cottonseed and oil-cake, but now I am dry they yoke me here, and give me refuse as fodder!"

The Brahman, still more sad, asked the road to give him its opinion. "My dear sir," said the road, "how foolish you are to expect anything else! Here am I, useful to everybody, yet all, rich and poor, great and small, trample on me as they go past, giving me nothing but the ashes of their pipes and the husks of their grain!"

At this the Brahman turned back sorrowfully; and on the way he met a Jackal, who called out, "Why, what's the matter, Mr Brahman? You look as miserable as a fish out of water!"

The Brahman told him all that had occurred. "How confusing!" said the Jackal, when the recital was ended. "Would you mind telling me over again, for everything was so mixed up?"

The Brahman told it all over again, but the Jackal shook his head in a distracted sort of way, and still could not understand.

"It's very odd," said he sadly, "but it all seems to go in at one ear and out at the other! I will go to the place where it all happened, and then, perhaps, I shall be able to give a judgement."

So they returned to the cage, by which the Tiger was waiting for the Brahman, and sharpening his teeth and claws.

"You've been away a long time!" growled the savage beast, "but now let us begin our dinner."

"*Our* dinner!" thought the wretched Brahman, as his knees knocked together with fright; "what a remarkably delicate way of putting it!"

"Give me five minutes, my lord!" he pleaded, "in order that I may explain matters to the Jackal here, who is somewhat slow in his wits."

The Tiger consented, and the Brahman began the whole story over again, not missing a single detail, and spinning as long a yarn as possible.

"Oh, my poor brain! Oh, my poor brain!" cried the Jackal, wringing its paws. "Let me see! how did it all begin? You were in the cage, and the Tiger came walking by –"

"Pooh!" interrupted the Tiger, "what a fool you are! I was in the cage."

"Of course!" cried the Jackal, pretending to tremble with fright; "yes! I was in the cage – no, I wasn't – dear! dear! where are my wits? Let me see – the Tiger was in the Brahman, and the cage came walking by – no, that's not it, either! Well, don't mind me, but begin your dinner, for I shall never understand!"

"Yes, you shall!" returned the Tiger, in a rage at the Jackal's stupidity. "I'll *make* you understand! Look here – I am the Tiger –"

"Yes, my lord!"

"And that is the Brahman –"

"Yes, my lord!"

"And that is the cage –"

"Yes, my lord!"

"And I was in the cage – do you understand?"

"Yes – no – Please, my lord –"

"Well?" cried the Tiger impatiently.

"Please, my lord! – how did you get in?"

"How! – why in the usual way, of course!"

"Oh, dear me! – my head is beginning to whirl again! Please don't be angry, my lord, but what is the usual way?"

At this the Tiger lost patience, and, jumping into the cage, cried, "This way! Now do you understand how it was?"

"Perfectly!" grinned the Jackal, as he dexterously shut the door, "and if you will permit me to say so, I think matters will remain as they were!"

THE CAT THAT WALKED BY HIMSELF

RUDYARD KIPLING

Whenever I read this story I hear my mother's voice. I must have been about six when she first read it to me. I used to know it off by heart – I still do in part. I milk cows most days of my life, and often think of the Man and the Woman who first milked a cow. I simply adore this story – and I'm getting on for sixty now. I don't throw boots at the cat, honestly; but I do love it when the dog chases him up a tree.

HEAR AND ATTEND AND LISTEN; for this befell and behappened and became and was, O my Best Beloved, when the Tame animals were wild. The Dog was wild, and the Horse was wild, and the Cow was wild, and the Sheep was wild, and the Pig was wild – as wild as wild could be – and they walked in the Wet Wild Woods by their wild lones. But the wildest of all the wild animals was the Cat. He walked by himself, and all places were alike to him.

Of course the Man was wild too. He was dreadfully wild. He didn't even begin to be tame until he met the Woman, and she told him that she did not like living in his wild ways. She picked out a nice dry Cave, instead of a heap of wet leaves, to lie down in; and she strewed clean sand on the floor; and she lit a nice fire of wood at the back of the cave; and she hung a dried wild-horse skin, tail-down, across the opening of the Cave; and she said, "Wipe your feet, dear, when you come in, and now we'll keep house."

That night, Best Beloved, they ate wild sheep roasted on the hot stones, and flavoured with wild garlic and wild pepper; and wild duck stuffed with wild rice and wild fenugreek and wild coriander; and marrow-bones of wild oxen; and wild cherries, and wild grenadillas. Then the Man went to sleep in front of the fire ever so happy; but the Woman sat up, combing her hair. She took the bone of the shoulder of mutton – the big flat blade-bone – and she looked at the wonderful marks on it, and she threw more wood on the fire, and she made a Magic. She made the First Singing Magic in the world.

Out in the Wet Wild Woods all the wild animals gathered together where they could see the light of the fire a long way off, and they wondered what it meant.

Then Wild Horse stamped with his wild foot and said, "O my Friends and O my Enemies, why have the Man and the Woman made that great light in that great Cave, and what harm will it do us?"

Wild Dog lifted up his wild nose and smelled the smell of the roast mutton, and said, "I will go up and see and look, and say; for I think it is good. Cat, come with me."

"Nenni!" said the Cat. "I am the Cat who walks by himself, and all places are alike to me. I will not come."

"Then we can never be friends again," said Wild Dog, and he trotted off to the Cave. But when he had gone a little way the Cat said to himself, "All places are alike to me. Why should I not go too and see and look and come away at my own liking?" So he slipped after Wild Dog softly, very softly, and hid himself where he could hear everything.

When Wild Dog reached the mouth of the Cave he lifted up the dried horse-skin with his nose and sniffed the beautiful smell of the roast mutton, and the Woman, looking at the blade-bone, heard him, and laughed, and said, "Here comes the first. Wild Thing out of the Wild Woods, what do you want?"

Wild Dog said, "O my Enemy and Wife of my Enemy, what is this that smells so good in the Wild Woods?"

Then the Woman picked up a roasted mutton-bone and threw it to Wild Dog, and said, "Wild Thing out of the Wild Woods, taste and try." Wild Dog gnawed the bone, and it was more delicious than anything he had ever tasted, and he said, "O my Enemy and Wife of my Enemy, give me another."

The Woman said, "Wild Thing out of the Wild Woods, help my Man to hunt through the day and guard this Cave at night, and I will give you as many roast bones as you need."

"Ah!" said the Cat, listening. "This is a very wise Woman, but she is not so wise as I am."

Wild Dog crawled into the Cave and laid his head on the Woman's lap, and said, "O my Friend and Wife of my Friend, I will help your Man to hunt through the day, and at night I will guard your Cave."

"Ah!" said the Cat, listening. "That is a very foolish Dog." And he went back through the Wet Wild Woods waving his wild tail, and walking by his wild lone. But he never told anybody.

When the Man waked up he said, "What is Wild Dog doing here?" And the Woman said, "His name is not Wild Dog any more, but the First Friend, because he will be our friend for always and always and always. Take him with you when you go hunting."

Next night the Woman cut great green armfuls of fresh grass from the water-meadows, and dried it before the fire, so that it smelt like new-mown hay, and she sat at the mouth of the Cave and plaited a halter out of horse-hide, and she looked at the shoulder-of-mutton bone – at the big broad blade-bone – and she made a Magic. She made the Second Singing Magic in the world.

Out in the Wild Woods all the wild animals wondered what had happened to Wild Dog, and at last Wild Horse stamped with his foot and said, "I will go and see and say why Wild Dog has not returned. Cat, come with me."

"Nenni!" said the Cat. "I am the Cat who walks by himself, and all places are alike to me. I will not come." But all the same he followed Wild Horse softly, very softly, and hid himself where he could hear everything.

When the Woman heard Wild Horse tripping and stumbling on his long mane, she laughed and said, "Here comes the second. Wild Thing out of the Wild Woods, what do you want?"

Wild Horse said, "O my Enemy and Wife of my Enemy, where is Wild Dog?"

The Woman laughed, and picked up the blade-bone and looked at it, and said, "Wild Thing out of the Wild Woods, you did not come here for Wild Dog, but for the sake of this good grass."

And Wild Horse, tripping and stumbling on his long mane, said, "That is true; give it me to eat."

The Woman said, "Wild Thing out of the Wild Woods, bend your wild head and wear what I give you, and you shall eat the wonderful grass three times a day."

"Ah," said the Cat, listening, "this is a very clever Woman, but she is not so clever as I am."

Wild Horse bent his wild head, and the Woman slipped the plaited hide halter over it, and Wild Horse breathed on the Woman's feet and said, "O my Mistress, and Wife of my Master, I will be your servant for the sake of the wonderful grass."

"Ah," said the Cat, listening, "that is a very foolish Horse." And he went back through the Wet Wild Woods, waving his wild tail and walking by his wild lone. But he never told anybody.

When the Man and the Dog came back from hunting, the Man said, "What is Wild Horse doing here?" And the Woman said, "His name is not Wild Horse any more, but the First Servant, because he will carry us from place to place for always and always and always. Ride on his back when you go hunting."

Next day, holding her wild head high that her wild horns should not catch in the wild trees, Wild Cow came up to the Cave, and the Cat followed, and hid himself just the same as before; and everything happened just the same as before; and the Cat said the same things as before; and when Wild Cow had promised to give her milk to the Woman every day in exchange for the wonderful grass, the Cat went back through the Wet Wild Woods waving his wild tail and walking by his wild lone, just the same as before. But he never told anybody. And when the Man and the Horse and the Dog came home from hunting and asked the same questions same as before, the Woman said, "Her name is not Wild Cow any more, but the Giver of Good Food. She will give us the warm white milk for always and always and always, and I will take care of her while you and the First Friend and the First Servant go hunting."

Next day the Cat waited to see if any other Wild Thing would go up to the Cave, but no one moved in the Wet Wild Woods, so the Cat walked there by himself; and he saw the Woman milking the Cow, and he saw the light of the fire in the Cave, and he smelt the smell of the warm white milk.

Cat said, "O my Enemy and Wife of my Enemy, where did Wild Cow go?"

The Woman laughed and said, "Wild Thing out of the Wild Woods, go back to the Woods again, for I have braided up my hair, and I have put away the magic blade-bone, and we have no more need of either friends or servants in our Cave."

Cat said, "I am not a friend, and I am not a servant. I am the Cat who walks by himself, and I wish to come into your Cave."

Woman said, "Then why did you not come with First Friend on the first night?"

Cat grew very angry and said, "Has Wild Dog told tales of me?"

Then the Woman laughed and said, "You are the Cat who walks by himself, and all places are alike to you. You are neither a friend nor a servant. You have said it yourself. Go away and walk by yourself in all places alike."

Then Cat pretended to be sorry and said, "Must I never come into the Cave? Must I never sit by the warm fire? Must I never drink the warm white milk? You are very wise and very beautiful. You should not be cruel even to a Cat."

Woman said, "I knew I was wise, but I did not know I was beautiful. So I will make a bargain with you. If ever I say one word in your praise, you may come into the Cave."

"And if you say two words in my praise?" said the Cat.

"I never shall," said the Woman, "but if I say two words in your praise, you may sit by the fire in the Cave."

"And if you say three words?" said the Cat.

"I never shall," said the Woman, "but if I say three words

in your praise, you may drink the warm white milk three times a day for always and always and always."

Then the Cat arched his back and said, "Now let the Curtain at the mouth of the Cave, and the Fire at the back of the Cave, and the Milk-pots that stand beside the Fire, remember what my Enemy and the Wife of my Enemy has said." And he went away through the Wet Wild Woods waving his wild tail and walking by his wild lone.

That night when the Man and the Horse and the Dog came home from hunting, the Woman did not tell them of the bargain that she had made with the Cat, because she was afraid they might not like it.

Cat went far and far away and hid himself in the Wet Wild Woods by his wild lone for a long time till the Woman forgot all about him. Only the Bat – the little upside-down Bat – that hung inside the Cave knew where Cat hid; and every evening Bat would fly to Cat with news of what was happening.

One evening Bat said, "There is a Baby in the Cave. He is new and pink and fat and small, and the Woman is very fond of him."

"Ah," said the Cat, listening, "but what is the Baby fond of?"

"He is fond of things that are soft and tickle," said the Bat. "He is fond of warm things to hold in his arms when he goes to sleep. He is fond of being played with. He is fond of all those things."

"Ah," said the Cat, listening, "then my time has come."

Next night Cat walked through the Wet Wild Woods and hid very near the Cave till morning-time, and Man and Dog and Horse went hunting. The Woman was busy cooking that morning, and the Baby cried and interrupted. So she carried him outside the Cave and gave him a handful of pebbles to play with. But still the Baby cried.

Then the Cat put out his paddy paw and patted the Baby on the cheek, and it cooed; and the Cat rubbed against its fat knees and tickled it under its fat chin with his tail. And the Baby laughed; and the Woman heard him and smiled.

Then the Bat – the little upside-down Bat – that hung in the mouth of the Cave said, "O my Hostess and Wife of my Host and Mother of my Host's Son, a Wild Thing from the Wild Woods is most beautifully playing with your Baby."

"A blessing on that Wild Thing whoever he may be," said the Woman, straightening her back, "for I was a busy woman this morning and he has done me a service."

That very minute and second, Best Beloved, the dried horse-skin Curtain that was stretched tail-down at the mouth of the Cave fell down – *whoosh!* – because it remembered the bargain she had made with the Cat; and when the Woman went to pick it up – lo and behold! – the Cat was sitting quite comfy inside the Cave.

"O my Enemy and Wife of my Enemy and Mother of my Enemy," said the Cat, "it is I: for you have spoken a word in my praise, and now I can sit within the Cave for always and always and always. But still I am still the Cat who walks by himself, and all places are alike to me."

The Woman was very angry, and shut her lips tight and took up her spinning-wheel and began to spin.

But the Baby cried because the Cat had gone away, and the Woman could not hush it, for it struggled and kicked and grew black in the face.

"O my Enemy and Wife of my Enemy and Mother of my Enemy," said the Cat, "take a strand of the thread that you are spinning and tie it to your spinning-whorl and drag it along the floor, and I will show you a Magic that shall make your Baby laugh as loudly as he is now crying."

"I will do so," said the Woman, "because I am at my wits' end; but I will not thank you for it."

She tied the thread to the little clay spindle-whorl and drew it across the floor, and the Cat ran after it and patted it with his paws and rolled head over heels, and tossed it backward over his shoulder and chased it between his hind legs and pretended to lose it, and pounced down upon it again, till the Baby laughed as loudly as it had been crying, and scrambled after the Cat and frolicked all over the Cave till it grew tired and settled down to sleep with the Cat in its arms.

"Now," said Cat, "I will sing the Baby a song that shall keep him asleep for an hour." And he began to purr, loud and low, low and loud, till the Baby fell fast asleep. The Woman smiled as she looked down upon the two of them, and said, "That was wonderfully done. No question but you are very clever, O Cat."

That very minute and second, Best Beloved, the smoke of the Fire at the back of the Cave came down in clouds from the roof – *puff!* – because it remembered the bargain she had made with the Cat; and when it had cleared away – lo and behold! – the Cat was sitting quite comfy close to the fire.

"O my Enemy and Wife of my Enemy and Mother of my Enemy," said the Cat, "it is I: for you have spoken a second word in my praise, and now I can sit by the warm fire at the back of the Cave for always and always and always. But still I am the Cat who walks by himself, and all places are alike to me."

Then the Woman was very very angry, and let down her hair and put more wood on the fire and brought out the broad blade-bone of the shoulder of mutton and began to make a Magic that should prevent her from saying a third word in praise of the Cat. It was not a Singing Magic, Best Beloved, it was a Still Magic; and by and by the Cave grew so still that a little wee-wee mouse crept out of a corner and ran across the floor.

"O my Enemy and Wife of my Enemy and Mother of my Enemy," said the Cat, "is that little mouse part of your magic?"

"Ouh! Chee! No indeed!" said the Woman, and she dropped the blade-bone and jumped upon the footstool in front of the fire and braided up her hair very quick for fear that the mouse should run up it.

"Ah," said the Cat, watching, "then the mouse will do me no harm if I eat it?"

"No," said the Woman, braiding her hair, "eat it quickly and I will ever be grateful to you."

Cat made one jump and caught the little mouse, and the Woman said, "A hundred thanks. Even the First Friend is not quick enough to catch little mice as you have done. You must be very wise."

That very moment and second, O Best Beloved, the Milk-pot that stood by the fire cracked in two pieces – *ffft!* – because it remembered the bargain she had made with the Cat; and when the Woman jumped down from the footstool – lo and behold! – the Cat was lapping up the warm white milk that lay in one of the broken pieces.

"O my Enemy and Wife of my Enemy and Mother of my Enemy," said the Cat, "it is I: for you have spoken three word in my praise, and now I can drink the warm white milk three times a day for always and always and always. But *still* I am the Cat who walks by himself, and all places are alike to me."

Then the Woman laughed and set the Cat a bowl of the warm white milk and said, "O Cat you are as clever as a man, but remember that your bargain was not made with the Man or the Dog, and I do not know what they will do when they come home."

"What is that to me?" said the Cat. "If I have my place in the Cave by the fire and my warm white milk three times a day I do not care what the Man or the Dog can do."

That evening when the Man and the Dog came into the Cave, the Woman told them all the story of the bargain, while the Cat sat by the fire and smiled. Then the Man said, "Yes, but he has not made a bargain with *me* or with all proper Men after me." Then he took off his two leather boots and he took up his little stone axe (that makes three) and he fetched a piece of wood and a hatchet (that is five altogether), and he set them out in a row and he said, "Now we will make *our* bargain. If you do not catch mice when you are in the Cave for always and always and always, I will throw these five things at you whenever I see you, and so shall all proper Men do after me."

"Ah," said the Woman, listening, "this is a very clever Cat, but he is not so clever as my Man."

The Cat counted the five things (and they looked very knobby) and he said, "I will catch mice when I am in the Cave for always and always and always; but *still* I am the Cat who walks by himself, and all places are alike to me."

"Not when I am near," said the Man. "If you had not said that last I would have put all these things away for always and always and always; but now I am going to throw my two boots and my little stone axe (that makes three) at you whenever I meet you. And so shall all proper Men do after me."

Then the Dog said, "Wait a minute. He has not made a bargain with *me* or with all proper Dogs after me." And he showed his teeth and said, "If you are not kind to the Baby while I am in the Cave for always and always and always, I will hunt you till I catch you, and when I catch you I will bite you. And so shall all proper Dogs do after me."

"Ah," said the Woman, listening, "this is a very clever Cat, but he is not so clever as the Dog."

Cat counted the Dog's teeth (and they looked very

pointed) and he said, "I will be kind to the Baby while I am in the Cave, as long as he does not pull my tail too hard, for always and always and always. But *still* I am the Cat that walks by himself, and all places are alike to me!"

"Not when I am near," said the Dog. "If you had not said that last I would have shut my mouth for always and always and always; but *now* I am going to hunt you up a tree whenever I meet you. And so shall all proper Dogs do after me."

Then the Man threw his two boots and his little stone axe (that makes three) at the Cat, and the Cat ran out of the Cave and the Dog chased him up a tree; and from that day to this, Best Beloved, three proper Men out of five will always throw things at a Cat whenever they meet him, and all proper Dogs will chase him up a tree. But the Cat keeps his side of the bargain too. He will kill mice, and he will be kind to Babies when he is in the house, just as long as they do not pull his tail too hard. But when he has done that, and between times, and when the moon gets up and night comes, he is the Cat that walks by himself, and all places are alike to him. Then he goes out to the Wet Wild Woods or up the Wet Wild Trees or on the Wet Wild Roofs, waving his wild tail and walking by his wild lone.

ACKNOWLEDGEMENTS

The publisher would like to thank the copyright holders for permission to reproduce the following copyright material:

James Berry: "Son-Son Fetches the Mule" from *The Future-Telling Lady* by James Berry (Hamish Hamilton, 1991). Copyright © James Berry 1991. Reproduced by permission of Penguin Books Ltd. **Geoffrey Dutton**: "The Wedge-Tailed Eagle" by Geoffrey Dutton. Reprinted by permission of the copyright owner, care of Curtis Brown (Aust) Pty Ltd. **Janet Frame**: "The Birds Began to Sing" from *The Lagoon and Other Stories* by Janet Frame. Copyright © Janet Frame 1951, 1991. Reproduced with permission of Curtis Brown Ltd, London, on behalf of Janet Frame. **Paul Gallico**: Extract from *The Snow Goose* by Paul Gallico. Copyright © 1941 by Paul Gallico. Reprinted by permission of Gillon Aitken Associates Ltd. **Ernest Hemingway**: Extract from *The Old Man and the Sea* by Ernest Hemingway (Jonathan Cape, 1952). Reprinted by permission of Random House UK Ltd and The Hemingway Foreign Rights Trust. **Barry Hines**: Extract from *A Kestrel for a Knave* (*Kes*) by Barry Hines (Michael Joseph, 1968). Copyright © Barry Hines 1968. Reproduced by permission of Penguin Books Ltd. **Ted Hughes**: Extract from *The Iron Woman* by Ted Hughes (Faber and Faber Ltd, 1993). Text copyright © Ted Hughes 1993. Used by permission of Faber and Faber Ltd. **The King James Bible**: Extracts from the Authorized Version of the Bible (The King James Bible), the rights in which are vested in the Crown, are reproduced by permission of the Crown's Patentee, Cambridge University Press. **Dick King-Smith**: Extract from *Godhanger* by Dick King-Smith. Copyright © Fox Busters Ltd 1996. Reprinted by permission of A. P. Watt Ltd on behalf of Fox Busters Ltd. **Rudyard Kipling**: "The Cat That Walked by Himself" from

Just So Stories by Rudyard Kipling. Reprinted by permission of A. P. Watt Ltd on behalf of The National Trust for Places of Historic Interest or Natural Beauty. **Beryl Markham**: "He Was a Good Lion" from *West With the Night* by Beryl Markham. Copyright © 1942, 1983 by Beryl Markham. Reprinted by permission of Laurence Pollinger Limited on behalf of the Estate of Beryl Markham. **Michael Morpurgo**: Extract from *Waiting for Anya* by Michael Morpurgo. Copyright © 1990 by Michael Morpurgo. Used by permission of Mammoth, an imprint of Egmont Children's Books Ltd, London. **John Steinbeck**: Extract from *The Red Pony* by John Steinbeck (William Heinemann, 1938). Text copyright © John Steinbeck 1938. Reprinted by permission of Random House UK Ltd. **E. B. White**: Extract from *Charlotte's Web* by E. B. White (Hamish Hamilton, 1952). Copyright © 1952 by J. White. Reproduced by permission of Penguin Books Ltd. **Henry Williamson**: Extract from *Tarka the Otter* by Henry Williamson (Bodley Head, 1965). Reprinted by permission of Random House UK Ltd.

Every effort has been made to obtain permission to reproduce copyright material but there may be cases where we have been unable to contact a copyright holder. The publisher will be happy to correct any omissions in future printings.